FOSSIL COVE PRESS

WHAT DEVOURS ALSO HUNGERS

A Short Story Collection

by

D. G. Valdron

WHAT DEVOURS ALSO HUNGERS

Table of Contents

Introduction

There is absolutely nothing interesting about me.
Sorry.

I kind of like it that way. I plan to keep it that way. So, sorry. I have nothing to say, and there's really nothing worth learning about me.

What I am, is an invisible presence, I'm a voice in your head. That's all I need to be.

Sometimes the voice is feverish and urgent. Sometimes my presence is calm and measured. I'm trains of words, images and ideas that you read. And if I'm very good at it, some of this will be with you after you've closed your eyes. Some of me will linger.

There are sixteen stories here. Stories of predators, the things that devour the things that are always hungry. There are fevered dreams of things outside reality, and there are encounters with the ruthless urges of serial killers. There's a tribute to H.P. Lovecraft, and pastiches of the faceless strangers of slasher movies. There is a story of an ultimate monster, and stories driven by love, by desire, by sex and reproduction.

These are stories of monsters and victims and heroes. Sometimes it's hard to tell which is which.

I have many stories, here and elsewhere.

If you've already read me, then welcome back.

And if this is your first, then I hope you will join me after this on more journeys to strange lands.

Join that voice that whispers in the night.

The Squad

An armoured limousine drives through the desert across an empty dirt road. A cloud of billowing dust rises up behind it. In the distance a series of guard towers loom. As we get closer we see that they're connected by three layers of cyclone fences and barbed wire. Ominous signs appear: "Trespassers will be executed." "Minefields Active." Powerful stadium lights illuminate the landscape beyond.

Cut to the inside of the armoured car. There are two people. The driver is ranked as a General. He's smoking a cigar. He's in his late fifties, prematurely gray and wrinkled. His passenger is a Lieutenant, clean cut, crisp, by the book, female and stern.

GENERAL -*This is all just for show. They throw money at us; we have to spend it on something. Worst goddamned duty in the service as far as I'm concerned, sitting in those towers waiting to be killed. Pushing paper at Checkpoint Charley. The real protection is distance. We've got another sixty miles to go. Sixty miles of the most godforsaken, desolate territory on the face of the earth. No water, no plants, not even a lizard can live here. We made sure of that. We got a geosynchronous satellite up there permanently stationed right over us, watching. I can't tell you what that cost us. A bird flies over this place, we know it. We got traps and deadfalls, minefields everywhere. Set a man down in here, and he's dead within a day.*

The Lieutenant looks doubtful.

GENERAL - *Distance is what it is. This car is wired to explode if anything happens. Those sons of bitches will have to walk out. They're a lot faster than they look, don't be fooled. But even they, take em most of a day to get out this far, takes them even longer to get anywhere. By that time, we can organize a response.*

LIEUTENANT -*Sounds like a tough set up.*

GENERAL - *Not tough enough. We almost had a break out in 1999. They decided to go for a walk, the whole bunch of them. Cut right through the fences as if it wasn't there, the minefields, the towers, didn't matter more than swatting flies.*

LIEUTENANT - *Briefing report says that they're all just psychopathic criminals. But my dossier doesn't tell me anything, just names and bullshit. Like this: "Likes teddy bears." What does that even mean? There's no psychological profiles, no personality assessments, just random notations. I expected the dirty dozen, but this.... There's no specialties identified, there's no history for any of them. I can't believe they're regular army.*

GENERAL - *They're not.*

LIEUTENANT - *Permission to speak freely sir?*

GENERAL - *There's just us here.*

LIEUTENANT - *This is fucked, Sir. What the hell am I supposed to be doing?*

GENERAL - *You lead them, Lieutenant. You take them out into the field, and you maybe try to point them, and then after, you try to get them to stop.*

LIEUTENANT - *Why me?*

GENERAL - *You're a woman. You fit a profile.*

LIEUTENANT - *So... What? They don't kill women?*

GENERAL - *They kill everyone and everything. Men, women, children, dogs, cattle. There ain't anything they don't kill. But sometimes, it looks like maybe they don't like to kill certain women. Or at least, they don't try as hard. Or maybe they can't. We're not sure.*

LIEUTENANT - *Who are these men?*

GENERAL - *They're not men.*

LIEUTENANT - *Then what? Martians? Aliens? Werewolves? Vampires? Genetic experiments?*

GENERAL - *No one really knows. They started showing up in the Eighties. Or at least, that's when we started noticing them. Then, the historians poked around, and whatever they are, that goes way back. But we're not sure. We don't know much about them. We know names, but that doesn't tell us anything. We know where each of them came from, sort of. We know what they've done. But what are they? You tell me after you meet them.*

LIEUTENANT - *What's the point of this?*

GENERAL - *You know the Iraq War, how Baghdad just fell apart? You heard of the Chinese Border incident, though we hushed that one up pretty good. That mess in Africa? Scottsboro? That's them. It's what they do. When things are really bad, alien invasion, vampire infestation, zombie outbreak, we send them in. And then...*

LIEUTENANT - *And then...*

GENERAL - *And then, Lieutenant? We pray.*

LIEUTENANT - *That they succeed?*

GENERAL - *No, Lieutenant. We pray that sooner or later, they stop.*

The Lieutenant looks out the window. There's no answer. The car proceeds in silence through the sterile and endless desert. They pass by a human skeleton half buried by the side of the road. The Lieutenant watches it as they go past.

* * *

The building looks like it was a gas station in the 1950's. The old fashioned gas pumps are still there, covered with dust. There is a drive through around the back. The General pulls up to the window. No one appears.

GENERAL - Checkpoint Charlie. The last stop before them.

There's an emphasis on the word 'them.' The Lieutenant doesn't respond. The General fishes out a clipboard and pen from the dash and makes a few notes. They wait. After a few minutes, the General honks the horn. Nothing. The General peers at the Clipboard.

GENERAL- They're on a nine day rotation. In, then out. After that, counselling, suicide watch, medication, whatever it takes. They're only six days in, should be fine.

Nothing. Abruptly the General guns the engine, pulls out to the front of the station and parks. For a moment, the motor idles, then he shuts it off.

LIEUTENANT - We're not supposed to exit the vehicle, Sir.

GENERAL - Whatever.

He puffs his cigar.

GENERAL - What are they going to do? Court martial us?

The General steps out of the vehicle, and the Lieutenant, impelled by some random feeling of solidarity, gets out with them. They walk over to the bay doors of the old garage. The windows are caked with decades of dust. The General wipes as best he can and stares in. Then he proceeds to the front door. The Lieutenant follows, but as he turns, she glimpses,

What Devours Also Hungers – Page 6

over his shoulder, four hanging bodies. The General strides through the front door, there's a counter, and beyond it, desks, telephones, piles of paper, all the detritus of a normal office. The General pounds on the counter and bellows.

Eventually an MP comes out from the back. He's got dried blood on his uniform, across his left shoulder, and spattering down the front of his shirt. He's got a crude bandage wrapped inexpertly around his temple. He is dishevelled, shirt untucked, buttons missing, fly unzipped. His eyes are a little wild.

GENERAL - *Paperwork.*

MP - *Ah, yes.*

The MP takes the clipboard, and starts leafing through it.

GENERAL - *There should be five men on station. Where are the others?*

MP - *They're around.*

GENERAL - *I saw them. What happened to you?*

MP - *Light fixture, Sir.*

GENERAL - *(nodding) - They can't take the weight. Maybe you were counting on getting electrocuted?*

MP - *Belts and suspenders, Sir. Make sure. Important to make sure. They wouldn't let us have guns. Not allowed anything sharp.*

The General grunts. The MP stamps a page.

MP - *Papers are in order, Sir.*

GENERAL - *Where were you when we came?*

MP – *Bathroom, Sir.*

The General shook his head.

GENERAL - *You're going to wreck the plumbing.*

MP - *The plumbing doesn't work, Sir. Nothing works. It's all just here. You can feel it every day. You can feel them from here. Like a stain. Like you're drowning in it.*

GENERAL - *You have three days left, Soldier, before relief.*

MP - *Yes, Sir.*

GENERAL - *Until you are relieved, you are not to kill yourself. Do you understand? That is an order.*

MP - *But General!*

GENERAL - *THAT'S AN ORDER! Not until you are relieved.*

The MP looks like he's about to break down and cry, a tear trickles down his cheek. He trembles, but in the end he salutes.

***

The armoured car pulls up on a ramshackle sprawling building. Shingles are peeled off the roof. The windows are broken. A door barely clings to its hinges.

GENERAL - *Used to be a residential compound for the Prometheus Project. This is all that's left.*

LIEUTENANT - *Prometheus?*

GENERAL - *Classified. Biological warfare. The next generation of superbugs, back when the world was simple and we knew who the bad guys were. Communists, blacks, hippies, that sort. Something got out, everyone died. I hear it was pretty messy. We dropped a neutron bomb to try and sterilize the place. We think we got most of it. At least, it hasn't spread much since then.*

LIEUTENANT - *So this is a biowarfare and a radiation hazard zone? And you station men here?*

What Devours Also Hungers – Page 8

GENERAL - *I told you before, they're not men.... We're here.*

The vehicle stops, in front of the building. A wind stirs through, but there's no motion. The windows are black. There's no sign of life. The General and the Lieutenant step out of the car. The Lieutenant looks around.

LIEUTENANT - *No sign of life. Maybe they're all dead, considering the place.*

GENERAL - *That's one theory to explain them.*

He hesitates.

GENERAL - *No sense wasting time, let's go in.*

The Lieutenant grabs her briefcase. The two proceed into the building. There is a large central hall, possibly a cafeteria. Tables and chairs are shattered or pushed to the side, light fixtures dangle from the ceiling. There are strange red splatters on the floor and walls. The place is empty. The two stand in the centre.

LIEUTENANT - *Where are they? They must have heard us coming? Were they informed?*

GENERAL - *Patience.*

From a darkened corridor, there's a series of heavy footsteps approaching closer and closer.

GENERAL - *It's them.*

The footsteps slow and heavy come louder and louder, but they can't see into the darkness. The Lieutenant draws closer to the General. Movement catches her eye; she looks behind them and screams. A hulking shape looms over them, a pale manikin's face atop military fatigues. Suddenly, they're surrounded by hulking, masked figures all around, bearing

primitive weapons. Axes, machetes, knives and clubs. All of
them unnaturally still and silent.

GENERAL - *Lieutenant, let me introduce you to your command:
Michaels, Jackson, Sawyer, Vernon, Hatcher, Beane, Monk, Otis, Ed
and Hatfield. Can't kill them; so we enlisted them.*

The Lieutenant turns around and around, staring at the
hulking passive figures, their attention focussed on her. As
she moves their heads track her.

LIEUTENANT - *They're all wearing masks.*

GENERAL - *Because they're all so damned ugly. Actually, some of
them, Michaels, Vernon, they look human. They could pass. But they
all like masks, it's some sort of pathology. They cover their faces, even
when there's no one to look. It's one of the little mysteries.*

The figures begin to gather, closing in on her.

LIEUTENANT - *Do they speak?*

GENERAL - *Sometimes one of them will say a word, so they can
speak. But they don't. The best you can hope for mostly is that they'll
listen sometimes.*

One of them, Vernon, reaches out a hand to touch the
Lieutenants hair. Trying not to show fear she moves away and
bumps into Hatcher. She retreats.

LIEUTENANT - *Get back! General, tell them to step back!*

The figures continue to close in on her.

GENERAL - *I said "sometimes" they listen. Sometimes. You're on
your own, Lieutenant. Consider this your test.*

The Lieutenant continues to back away, turning from one to
the other as they close in on her. Then she stops and visibly
gathers herself.

LIEUTENANT - I have something in my briefcase. (Announcing, clear commanding voice)

They stop, expectant. Not so much dissuaded as curious. A couple of them tilt their heads. Finally, one shrugs and they advance. The Lieutenant holds up her briefcase and snaps the lock, opening it towards her. Again, they hesitate for a second. She spins the briefcase around, so it faces them.

It contains a teddy bear.

LIEUTENANT - I brought this all this way. Who wants it?

She lowers the briefcase, which is otherwise empty, and holds the bear out. A broad heavy shape wearing a leather mask made of human skin, Sawyer, shambles forward. It reaches out.

LIEUTENANT - You want this?

She pulls the bear away from Sawyer. She stares directly at him. Sawyer is still. The others watch. The two stare at each other. Finally, Sawyer nods. The Lieutenant holds the teddy bear out to him. Sawyer takes it, and clutching it to him protectively, shambles off.

Jackson, the largest of them, advances towards her. But suddenly, Michaels the tallest, is in his path. Jackson pauses and tilts his head. Michaels tilts his head as if in answer. For a second, the moment hangs. And then, as if there was nothing, Jackson and Michaels walk off smoothly in different directions. In an instant, the rest of them have vanished. Not disappeared, but just... it's as if they'd all just casually walked away while she wasn't paying attention. But she had been watching.

GENERAL - Congratulations.

LIEUTENANT - I passed a test?

GENERAL - *They let you live. Come on, let's get out of here. The place gives me the creeps.*

They walk out to the car. The Lieutenant gets in, slams the door shut, she's shaking visibly.

LIEUTENANT - *My god, what are they!*

GENERAL - *I've got the papers for your first mission here. Read it, we've got the Evac Chopper coming. I'll be driving back.*

LIEUTENANT - *What are they?*

GENERAL - *There's some sort of outbreak over on the pacific coast. We've got a perimeter, but nothing we've sent in comes out. You're going to have to take them in.*

LIEUTENANT - *I SAID WHAT THE HELL ARE THEY???*

GENERAL - *I DON'T KNOW. NO ONE DOES!*

LIEUTENANT - *I thought they were going to kill me.*

GENERAL - *It was possible.*

LIEUTENANT - *And if they had?*

GENERAL - *Then I'd have brought someone else and hoped for the best.*

LIEUTENANT - *I'm not the first am I*

GENERAL - *You've got a mission coming up fast. You need to get your head around that.*

LIEUTENANT - *How many?*

There was a long pause.

GENERAL – Six.

LIEUTENANT - Six?

The General doesn't reply. The Lieutenant shoves him.

LIEUTENANT - *You brought six others? I'm the seventh?*

GENERAL - *Yes. One at a time.*

LIEUTENANT – *And?*

GENERAL (shrugs) - *They killed them. Each of them. It wasn't pretty. They like to take their time.*

LIEUTENANT - *And me...*

GENERAL - *You were the one. The one we were looking for.*

LIEUTENANT - *Why?*

GENERAL - *Because they let you live. You were the one. We don't know why. We don't know how they think. We don't know if they do think. We don't know why they do what they do. We don't know why they kill. We don't know why they let some live. We don't know how to kill them. We don't know how to stop them. If we did, we'd stop them. If we could, we'd kill them. But we can't. We can't even contain them for long. The best we can do is find someone they won't kill on sight and sort of direct them... point them at something that needs killing and then try and get out of the way.*

LIEUTENANT - *My God.*

GENERAL - *God has nothing to do with it. Here's how it is, they let you live, so they are yours now, and you are theirs. That's all. Now you've got your mission, get prepared.*

LIEUTENANT - *What about you? They let you live.*

GENERAL - *I was the last person they let live, until you came along.*

LIEUTENANT - *So why me?*

The General stares at her. Finally, he looks out the window.

GENERAL - *T-Cell Lymphoma. Inoperable. No treatment. I have maybe another month or two.*

LIEUTENANT - So... I'm your replacement.

The General nods.

GENERAL - We had to find someone they wouldn't kill. I'm sorry, it's a nightmare. But they're our nightmares, and there's others out there, bad things. We need-"

The bulletproof glass on the driver's side shatters, and Michaels and Vernon pull the General screaming out through the broken window. He kicks wildly, screaming in terror. The Lieutenant shouts, grabbing his feet. Her face is already flecked with his blood. They drag the General off.

The Lieutenant jumps out of the armoured car, shouting. She pulls her sidearm and empties it into Michaels and Vernon, but they don't seem to notice. She follows a half-dozen steps. As the General vanishes into the darkness of the building, her nerve breaks and she runs back to the car, slamming the door, futilely locking it. Praying to herself.

Inside the building, the General's screams go on and on and on....

On the seat beside her, the mission papers are scattered around.

The End

The Hold

Cordell Baker unzipped his fly, and with a few deft movements, casually began to urinate on his wife's grave.

Expressionlessly, he watched the hot stream burrow tiny ridges in the freshly turned brown earth.

Only the carved face of his wife, Elspeth, looked on. They were alone in the sunny afternoon. Elspeth's wish had always been to be buried, not in a cemetery, but on the farm she had grown up on.

"We're part of it, Cord," he could hear her voice, "and this land, its part of us."

She was part of the land now, he reflected. Part and parcel with it. Insensate rotting meat, slowly mixing it's atoms with the idiot soil. He had never really looked at the world in Elspeth's quasi-mystical way. You were born. You died. That was all.

He shook it carefully; a few drops falling on the headstone, and tucked it back in. He zipped up his fly.

He searched his mind for grief, and wasn't particularly surprised not to find any. Perhaps there was only room in Cordell's mind for Cordell. Everything else was just objects. Accessories to his life.

"You're like a cat, Cord," one of his lovers in town had said to him, as he'd lay back in bed and watched her with empty eyes. "Just like a cat. Like an animal. You don't care about anything at all."

That animal quality had always attracted women. Even Elspeth, back when they were kids growing up together. It was a calm self centeredness that wasn't quite ambition.

Had Elspeth known about his lovers? He wondered suddenly. If she had, it hadn't mattered. She had loved him with the unswerving dedication that had marked her life.

Moved by a sudden impulse, he reached out and put his hand on the tombstone. The feel of sun heated marble sent tingles through his palm.

Elspeth, he thought, I'm sorry that you died.

And in a way, he really was.

She'd been out with the tractor when it rolled over into an irrigation ditch; she'd been caught underneath it.

He'd come along a few minutes later, seen her pleading eyes; seen the blood soaking into the mud.

Cordell had calmly walked back to the house. Taking off his boots to avoid tracking mud into the kitchen, he'd made himself a pot of tea. Sitting there, alone in the kitchen, with the radio playing softly in the next room, he'd slowly drunk two cups of tea. Then he got up, cleaned out the teapot, put his boots back on, and went back out to see her.

She was dead by that time, of course.

"My family's blood is in this land, Cord," she'd said to him when they married.

Well, he reflected, hers certainly is now.

It had been her family's farm for generations. Elspeth had been the last surviving child, so it had gone to her.

And now to Cord.

Shifting his feet, Cord leaned forward, supporting his weight against the tombstone. He almost pulled away...

And now it would be sold. Cord was pleased, he'd get a good price for it, a far better price than he could have ever made by simply working the land.

The insurance settlement, his lawyer had assured him, would also be substantial. Between the two of them, Cord could probably not have to worry about ever working again.

Not that Cord was the kind of man to go through that kind of money quickly. Or the kind of man who would seriously contemplate not working. People found Cordell a sober, thrifty, reliable person, and that was largely a true impression. He seldom got drunk, and with the exception of a few whores on trips to the big city, rarely indulged any vice.

He straightened and almost walked off, but his attention returned to the tombstone. He flexed his fingers against the warm marble.

It almost felt like her, it almost felt like warm skin. But hard, like stone, not the soft of flesh.

He couldn't take his hand off the tombstone.

The thought startled him.

Some sort of misplaced remorse?

No, he was not the sort of person to be troubled by remorse. He didn't consider himself responsible for her death. That had been her own doing.

Or, if you wanted to split hairs, it was God's doing.

Perhaps he could have done something. Pried her crushed body out from under the tractor; somehow stopped the bleeding; taken her the fifteen miles to the hospital.

Perhaps, if he could have done all that and kept her alive. The Doctors might have been able to save her life; what there was of it, in an irreparably crippled body.

He doubted it.

Cordell pulled. He jerked his arm. It wouldn't come free.

Almost ludicrously, it occurred to him that this was some kid's stupid prank. They'd smeared crazy glue or something all over the stone and waited for him to touch it. For a leering moment he was irrationally glad he hadn't somehow decided to press his penis against the stone.

The little bastards, he thought, pulling that stunt and sitting back to laugh at you. He turned, looking around him as much as his trapped hand allowed. There was no one there.

A fly landed briefly on the headstone and took off again.

No, he told himself, if there was glue or something on the marble, you'd be able to see it. And it would have already set in the first few minutes it had been applied. It wouldn't be waiting there like a trap.

Like a trap.

The thought nosed around the back of his mind, like a dog looking for scraps. He booted it out.

Again he pulled, twisting his body hard. The shock travelled down his arm, to his wrist and then stopped.

He was still holding the damned stone. Beneath his hand was her face, her birth and death dates, and the dedication. Elspeth Baker, he couldn't let her go.

The thought made him laugh out loud suddenly. He quickly squelched the laugh. There wasn't anyone else around on the farm, but you never knew who might come to visit, or when. It wouldn't do to be seen laughing over your wife's grave.

Everyone had, after all been properly sympathetic over his loss. No one, not even the sheriff, who seemed habitually suspicious, had even hinted at wrongdoing. Everyone had understood his announced decision to sell out and leave.

How could anyone, they asked themselves, bear to work a farm that had killed his wife?

He pulled again, jerking hard. For a second, he almost felt his shoulder pop, then it settled back into place. He grunted.

They would say that this was something psychological. Some part of him refusing to give up the land.

Pull. Grunt.

It wasn't his land. It was Elspeth's.

Pull. Grunt.

All right then, refusing to give up Elspeth.

Pull. Grunt. Nothing.

But he knew himself better than that. He'd been happy to be with Elspeth, when she was here. But she was gone. Time to move on.

Pull. Grunt. Nothing.

His feet kicked up furrows in the bare earth covering her grave, scuffed dirt to cover the urine damped soil.

He panted. He almost leaned up against the headstone, but at the last minute, thought better of it.

All right, he told himself, this has to be something natural.

Like during the winter, sticking your tongue to a piece of cold metal railing. He'd done that once to himself as a boy. His mother had had to free him by carefully pouring hot water on the pipe.

After that he'd been regaled with horror stories about boys who'd torn the skin off their tongues that way.

He tried lifting off gently, working individual fingers loose with his free hand.

That didn't work. They seemed solidly affixed.

The sound of cars passing by came to him. Sound carried well out here, and he was out of sight of the road. But it wasn't that far off and people were continually coming to visit, to console his loss.

Cordell began to yell as he jerked and tried to pull himself from the tombstone. He was shocked by how quickly they took on the frenzied dimensions of a trapped animal. Scream piled on top of scream until his voice began to rasp. Raw throated, he continued to scream, pulling more and more wildly until he had the stone rocking back and forth. Finally with one desperate effort he managed to pull it up and over a few inches, until it leaned dizzily to one side.

That stopped him.

How much did this thing weigh?

Four or five hundred pounds, and sunk two feet into the ground for stability.

He was practically pulling it out. That was pretty much impossible even if he'd had a good grip, not this flat palm on the marble.

He should have torn the skin off his hand with that effort, if it was just stuck there. Just like the skinned tongues of childhood nightmares.

Instead, the tombstone had stayed fixed to his hand as he'd tried to pull the whole mess clear of the earth.

Panting, he waited a few minutes to catch his breath, and then bent down carefully for a good look.

There was no dividing line, none at all.

The pink flesh of his hand seamlessly merged with the pale marble of the stone.

Were his fingers flatter? It almost looked as if his hand was slowly sinking into the stone. That was insane.

The realization brought a new round of screaming and heaving. Throat aching, he yelled and yelled, with rasping cries as the stone rocked back and forth in small arcs. Only the physical pop of his shoulder being torn out of joint ended this tirade.

Cordell was on his knees gasping for breath, trying to collect his thoughts. He was quite careful not to let any other part of his body touch the stone.

He had to get free. That was the thought that occupied him now. He had to get free. It had an almost physical force. He no longer thought about why he was trapped, or how, or even if his neighbours saw him. He wanted free.

He searched his pockets. Wallet, money, coins, credit card, lint, washers, a piece of string, receipts, random pieces of paper. Useless. He let them fall at his feet.

In his back right pocket... The effort of reaching it caused his shoulder to flare. Cordell grit his teeth and reached anyway. There was a small mother of pearl handled jackknife. Three blades. The longest about four and a half inches long.

Not much of an edge.

Good for cutting twine, or scraping out the inside of a hoof, not much else.

It was all he had. Cordell set the knife body between his teeth and opened the blade with his free hand.

Gingerly Cordell probed along his trapped fingers, digging carefully, not wanting to cut himself unnecessarily.

He couldn't cut himself at all.

Where the fingers merged with the marble they were as solid and impervious as the marble itself. Only along the tops of the fingers did it feel like human flesh.

Cordell absorbed this information with wide eyes. Then, with the animal fatalism that had been the hallmark of his life, he stuck the knife into the ground between his feet and proceeded to unlace his boots.

He had to get free.

Again, it was hard to do it with one hand, but he managed. Tying the two bootlaces together he wound it around and around his wrist just above the trapped hand. He used his teeth to pull it tight as his free hand worked a makeshift knot.

He was ready now.

Not thinking about it. Not daring to think about it. Cordell picked up the knife and shoved it between the bones of his wrist just below the makeshift tourniquet.

A raw scream tore through him as the knife poked out the other side of his wrist. Bare nerves touched steel and sent staggering fire shooting back up his arm.

He had to get free. That was all he could allow himself to think of. He tried to keep his mind on the goal, as he began to saw through the cartilage and ligaments that held his wrist together.

Again and again the pain staggered him. There was a lot more blood than he expected, it spurted and trickled, splotching the pink marble. Red haze enveloped his eyes until he was afraid he'd pass out. At some point his bowels loosed in a warm rush down his overalls. But he kept at it, stabbing and gouging and tearing at his own flesh until it abruptly gave way.

Suddenly, Cordell was sitting back on his ass on the naked dirt of the gravemound, holding a stump with one hand, and looking at his other hand, still holding onto the tombstone.

It seemed so natural, resting there, that it almost looked like an optical trick. It looked like there should be an arm and a body attaching to that hand, sitting so pretty on the tombstone.

Then, as he watched, the pink marble tombstone slowly absorbed the hand into itself. The bloody wrist stump followed the fingers down, until it too was lost inside the stone.

My blood, he noticed, has vanished. All the blood he'd spilled getting free had also disappeared. As if it had been washed off the stone.

Or absorbed into it.

Elspeth's face, carved into relief on the surface of the stone, above her name, seemed to smile.

Did the stonemason put that expression on her? He wondered dizzily.

Cordell was very dizzy. Almost sleepy.

He allowed his head to dip, until he saw the stump at the end of his arm. It was still bleeding. Red drops made black mud in the earth between his legs.

Cordell forced himself to his feet and began lurching toward the house some thirty yards away. The animal urge to survive drove him on. He had to get to the house to live. At the house he could stop the bleeding. He could call for help.

Make up a story about an accident. Maybe even drive out himself. He needed to get to the house.

Nothing to it, he thought, just a few trees and a fence in the way.

Cordell staggered forward.

Halfway to the house, Cordell stopped, leaning against a tree, putting his hand out to support himself. He cradled the stump against his stomach, feeling its warm red pulse against his belly. Taking three deep breaths, he looked up toward the house.

Practically there, he told himself.

With a grunt of effort he straightened and tried to lurch forward again.

He couldn't.

Despairingly, he looked at the tree he'd walked past ten thousand times without a thought. The tree that had him caught.

Just above where his hand touched the tree, there was the outline of a heart scarred into the bark. A stylized arrow pierced it.

"E x C" she'd carved into the heart all those years ago when they'd been courting.

The human part of Cordell despaired in that moment, but deep down, that untouched and untouching primal core, the reptilian crocodile remnant of his brain drove him on.

Whimpering, he bent forward, bringing his trapped wrist within range of his bared teeth.

The End

Piggyback

It was purest luck that they caught the Strawberry Strangler alive, Gage reflected. A lot of the time, these guys tended to be killed resisting arrest. That simplified things.

Gage didn't care. Perhaps he'd cared once, when he'd joined the task force. But an unending diet of pure horror, like being force fed vomit, had abraded human sensibilities.

As horror went, the Strawberry Strangler was a pretty mundane one. Eleven murders over a year and a half. Basic sexual violations culminating in forcible asphyxiation by shoving foreign objects down the windpipe. Half of the victims had gagged and suffocated on their own vomit. The first acknowledged victim, actually the fourth, had been found in strawberry field. Hence the picturesque name.

The murderer didn't merit it. Gage had been in charge of the background check.

The killer was in his early twenties. A local boy who'd graduated high school and stagnated, full of promise gone wrong. Lazy and self-centred. A picture of narcissism.

This was what evil was, Gage had learned. Just a void. A hollow empty space, looking out through bovine eyes; slack-jawed droolers taking pathetic revenge on a too vulnerable world.

No evil geniuses. No Hannibal Lectors. Just shallow, stupid venality.

* * *

They sat in the room smoking cigarettes. Carl Darryl was chained to the chair, but they'd allowed his hands free so he could smoke a cigarette or have a coffee.

In one corner of the room sat a camcorder on a tripod, cables feeding into a portable hard drive. The Detectives were careful not to obscure its view of the murderer.

He was confessing. Sometimes they did that. After all the horror, they would sit there and casually recount their deeds. Glorying in it one last time. Sharing intimate secrets.

Carl was comfortable.

"They're all sluts," he told them, "I started breaking into houses in high school. I'd go through their drawers. You wouldn't believe what I'd find. Dildos and vibrators, handcuffs and nipple clamps. They'd be walking down the streets, acting like ladies. But they were all whores."

"Sometimes I'd come in their panties, and put it right back in the drawer. I wouldn't take anything. Sometimes I'd wonder if they ever knew, if any of them ever noticed."

"After a while, it wasn't enough..."

Carl graduated to rapes. Regardless of his views, he'd been remarkably unselective. By his own account, he'd taken housewives and grandmothers, children and teenagers, pretty girls and ugly ones. He was equal opportunity in his hatred.

"I liked to be in their homes, waiting for them..."

There was an obscene gleam in his eye.

There were fifteen reported rapes attributable to him, going back four years. He claimed many more. Some of his victims, he was sure, recognized him. He took their silence as approval.

"Susan West," the first victim. "I was waiting for her when she got home. She had this huge dildo in her panty drawer, you should have seen it. I made her deep throat it, and she did it too. Then I started on her. She got to choking; I felt her bucking and heaving. It was scary, but it felt real good. Afterwards, I took it with me. She wasn't moving when I left, but I hadn't figured she'd died or anything."

Carl grinned in an 'aw shucks' sort of way.

"I got really scared when I found out the next day. I hadn't meant for it to happen. I felt kind of bad."

"The next time, I was careful. I used the dildo on her throat again. She wasn't as good as Susan, she couldn't take it. She started choking right away. I beat her good with it, but I made sure she lived."

The next victim hadn't been so lucky.

"I just liked it better that way…"

The pattern had been set. In the strawberry field, the Dildo had been replaced by a rough stick of wood, splinters gouging the throat lining. Lisa Molloy had choked on her own blood. He'd strangled her for good measure.

As always, Gage marvelled at the impassionate nature of the telling. Darryl could have been talking about lawnmower repair. Only every once in a while did something flash through, as he described some particular degradation, some desperate plea. A sick reptilian satisfaction would leach out.

Evey Bonner, the eighth victim: "No, I never touched her. That was just some copycat. Nothing to do with me."

Marianne Mosley, the tenth victim: "I was drunk that night. Guess I must have inspired some fans."

All the others, he admitted to happily.

But not those two.

* * *

"Why those two?" Gage asked his partner.

It was late at night. They sat equidistant from a waste basket in the corner of the office, heaving crumpled wads of paper at it.

"Who knows? Maybe they were cousins or something. Or maybe they were nice to him in grade four. Maybe he was buddies with someone from one of their families. It doesn't matter, they both fit right into his profile. Motive, pattern, opportunity. He can play all the games he wants, we've got him."

What Devours Also Hungers – Page 27

"He might have an alibi for the Mosley killing. I think I should check it out."

"I doubt if it'll hold up. But go ahead."

* * *

"He was still there when I came in, in the morning," said Gary, the Bartender. "I'd of figured that one of his friends would have taken him home, but they hadn't."

"You're sure he was out of it?"

"I kicked him a few times to wake him up, not hard or anything, mind you. Then I let him into the can to clean up. He was a mess."

"Could he have gone out and then returned to that spot?"

The bartender laughed.

"I saw dried puke on his face from the night before. He was so drunk, he'd messed his clothes the night before. When I found him in the morning, he was still wearing them. If he could have gone anywhere, the first thing he would have done would be to get out of them."

"Do you remember when this was?"

"Sure, it was the night after the Fair opened. The day before they found that poor Mosley girl."

"Thanks, you've been a great help."

* * *

Establishing the time of death was an imprecise science at best. The human body showed great flexibility in its rates of corruption.

Marianne Mosley had last been seen alive, dancing with local boys at the Hoedown until 2:00 am. She'd been found six hours later. The body had been hidden in a cool dry tool shed. It had only been luck that the body had been found so quickly. Otherwise, it might have been a day or two before it was found.

What Devours Also Hungers – Page 28

The Bartender's story was corroborated by other witnesses: Patrons at the bar. The owner of the Boarding House where Darryl had stayed.

If this was accepted, then Darryl simply didn't have the opportunity to perform this killing.

If so, then there had to be a second murderer.

* * *

Smith had been unimpressed.

"So nobody actually saw him during the crucial times. All you have is some wet pants and dried puke, and a couple of witnesses who admit that they weren't interested in looking too close. All he had to do was change his clothes a couple of times."

"I think it's a little more than that," Gage said.

Smith shrugged.

"I don't see it. But if you want to follow this one, I'll back you up on it."

* * *

Two months had passed since the Strawberry Stranglers capture. The task force had been assigned to other cases. Nevertheless, Gage had returned to interview Darryl twice more.

The man was still adamant that he had not committed two of the killings.

Gage carefully watched the reports from the town. There were no further murders. No disappearances. Not even sexual assaults that might have fit the pattern.

The texts on pathological murders suggested that once the subjects began killing, they didn't stop. This had appeared to stop dead, with the one murder.

Or two, if Darryl was to be believed. He denied a second murder.

What was this then? A spur of the moment murder of passion, made to look like the Strawberry Strangler? He didn't think so. It was too...planned. And what about the second murder?

A second serial killer in the shadow of the first? If so, why stop with two? Why hadn't there been a follow up? Had he moved on? Was he somewhere else?

Gage chewed his pencil, and then typing rapidly, released a regional bulletin seeking reports of incidents which might fit a loose profile. Maybe something would turn up.

* * *

Nothing turned up.

Three months later, Soames, who'd abducted and murdered some twenty street kids in Detroit, was granted a new trial.

Gage and Smith had been at the centre of that investigation. They sat down with the District Attorney.

"It doesn't matter," he told them, "that we get him on all counts. He'll fry for one as easy as he fries for twenty. Give me the best cases, the surest best evidence."

"We'll go through the files," Smith assured him, "you'll have what you need."

* * *

Ultimately, they settled on five cases.

Incidents where witnesses saw him with the kids just before they vanished. Other witnesses placed him near where the bodies were found. Personal property of the deceased was found in his possession, grisly little trophies, in one case, a medallion, in another an actual fingernail. There were good casts of bite marks, semen and saliva samples, DNA.

In the case of one victim, he'd actually told a drinking buddy what he planned to do; it had seemed like a grisly joke at the time.

There were also four anomalous cases.

Gage found himself spending more and more time on them, although they'd clearly been excluded from prosecution in the preliminary reviews.

No witnesses. That of course, wasn't particularly probative. These guys tried to avoid witnesses.

No semen.

No saliva.

Bite marks in two of the cases, but the bites had been so badly mangled that it was impossible to get a match.

They were all at the high end of Soames preferred age range.

Even opportunity was speculative, Soames didn't seem to have been in the right places at the right times.

Burial sites were anomalous.

But they fit the profile. They followed the profile very closely. If not, Gage realized, for the evidence of the other murders, there was nothing to link these killings to Soames.

Gage discussed his concerns with Smith.

* * *

"This is like the Strawberry thing?" Smith said, after listening patiently.

Gage nodded.

"Something like that, maybe."

"A pathological killer whose modus operandi is a perfect match for a known and active killer, and who, once that killer is found, just stops." Smith's precise voice dripped with irony.

"Maybe he just switches modes," Gage suggested.

"Then we should be seeing something else. Anything else."

Abruptly, Smith reached across his desk, shuffling files, until he pulled out a folder. He handed it to Gage.

"Remember her?" He asked. "She could practically be another one of your anomalies. Except, except do you remember where we found her nipples?"

"I remember," Gage said, handing the file back, "she isn't one of the anomalous ones."

They stared at each other.

"We can't rule out a copycat," Smith said finally. "That's why we don't release all the information, to distinguish copycats from the real things. But I just can't see it as likely. Remember Occam's Razor."

"The simplest solution, ninety nine per cent of the time, is the correct one," Gage quoted. "But I've just got this gut feeling."

"Then go with it then," Smith counselled, "the worst thing that can happen is you'll waste some time. Big deal. You might turn up something. But..."

"What?" Gage prompted.

"Be careful. It would be embarrassing to the department, to the task force, if it turned out that we'd missed a killer along the way. If you're going to bring a case forward, make sure it's a damned good one. Otherwise they'll fry your ass, and mine too."

* * *

Nothing turned up that could be linked to the Strawberry killings. There was no new evidence on the Soames files.

Soames lost his trial again, and was duly sentenced to death. The District Attorney attended at the task force offices personally with a bottle of champagne.

Eventually, Gage moved on. There were current files to work on, after all.

Still, the experiences with Soames and Darryl had left him with a feeling of uncertainty. Once the killer was caught, the task force generally stopped looking.

"What's left to look for?" he could hear Smith's mocking reply.

He began to look through some of the other closed files. Looking for anomalies. Looking for killings, that the murderers might not have committed.

The trouble with anomalies was that they were anomalous. They didn't have any rules.

Darryl had admitted to nine, but denied two. Soames had denied all of them, but four didn't quite fit.

A man nicknamed Strangler Bill, William Beaudine, claimed to have killed forty-two people. One for every year of his life. Beaudine was a pathological liar. Estimates of his real count varied among law enforcement agencies, between nineteen and twenty-five being attributed to him.

Did that make for six anomalies?

* * *

Still, it seemed to add up. Gage found that on almost every serial killer file the task force had worked on, there was always at least one or two murders that didn't quite add up.

Gage recognized that he was beginning to obsess. Smith helped where he could; signing files out for Gage, conducting reviews. Sometimes, Smith would come up with his own anomalies, and they would argue about it over a beer.

His regular work began to slide. Smith covered for him as best he could, which did little more than earn a verbal reprimand. Gage began to notice the other co-workers starting to whisper about him. Smith defended him to the others, but privately was becoming increasingly concerned.

The picture that Gage found himself painting appalled him. A whole nation of hidden killers, of secondary Dahmers and Gacys. The task force as bungling incompetents, dropping the ball again and again. He had to reject it.

And yet...

There were at least forty-three anomalies.

* * *

It was a beautiful spring day. They were all gathered at the Office, collating data on a series of roadside execution style killings across seven states. Odds are that they had identified another serial killer.

Smith sat down beside his desk.

"I've been thinking about these anomalies," Smith said. "It doesn't make sense. Pathological killings that just stop, these people can't just stop. And they're too close to be copycats; copycats, random civilians just wouldn't have that kind of knowledge. Case by case, it just doesn't work."

"But if you look at them as a group..." Gage began.

"Yes," Smith said quickly, "look at them as a group. Then it starts to make a kind of sense. Then, it's as if the pathological killings aren't just stopping. They just keep moving on.

"And the thing with copycats is... Maybe a copycat would have the right information, to make it look like someone else...if they were in the right place. It always comes down to the simplest solution."

"What are you saying?" Gage asked. "That there's a piggyback killer riding the others? That he'd have to be with the police? Who knows, maybe even the task force?"

A cold chill ran down his back.

Who could they trust?

"All the anomalies," Smith whispered, "are in files that you've been on."

"That's not right," Gage whispered, shocked. There were anomalies on files he'd hardly connected with. He cast his mind back, desperately searching.

"Give me your badge," Smith whispered urgently.

"What?" he said, reaching automatically into his jacket for it.

From behind him, he heard a shout. "Watch it! He's going for his gun!"

"What?" he said turning and standing.

"Look out," someone else screamed.

From the corner of his eye he saw Smith diving to the floor. He saw the red wound on his chest, just before he heard the shot ring out.

Someone shot me, he thought, as his knees buckled.

Gage passed out.

* * *

"Jesus Christ, I shot him," he heard a voice saying. "I worked next to him for five years."

Gage coughed, he couldn't seem to breathe properly. His chest bubbled and he spat up blood.

He was on the floor, stretched out. He felt someone's arms around him, holding him.

"He was going for his gun," Smith's voice, tinged with disbelief. "One minute I'm just talking to him about it, it was too crazy to be true. I expected him to laugh. Then he's going for his gun and all I can think is I don't believe it, I'm going to die, and I can't believe it."

"...A fucking disaster, a complete fucking disaster. When this gets out, they're going to clean house, we'll be lucky to get jobs guarding parking lots." Gage recognized the Captain's voice.

"Thirty, maybe forty, piggybacking along. Slipping a couple of extra killings into every investigation. He was the one that found those nipples, wasn't he? After the regular squads had been through twice."

"I was there with him for that," Smith's voice protested. "I mean, sometimes things just turn up, you don't think anything of it."

Abruptly he felt a hard kick in his side.

"Bastard!" a voice screamed.

"Enough of that," a harsh voice warned. "How's he doing?"

"Lungs filling with blood, he's not going to make it to the ambulance. How many files do you think we're going to have to reopen?"

"We're not reopening any files."

"But Sir..."

"Forget it. The files are closed, the murders are attributed. I'm not going to take a chance on animals like Soames walking just because we might connect some of those him. Ever hear of reasonable doubt? If this gets out, every single one of those bastards, every case he ever worked, will be filing appeals. Besides, I don't think we'll have much luck pinning anything on this fucker, not after all this time."

"That's a cover up, Sir," he could hear Smith's voice protesting.

"No it's not a cover up; it's a potential fucking bottomless pit. We can all fucking disappear down it, and frankly, I don't intend to go. All we got are suspicions. The files stay closed, and we let this one go. Let's bury the bastard with honours. At least it'll be over."

"But we shot him, Sir," Smith complained.

"We'll deal with that. Call it a tragic accident."

Smith looked down at him for a second, and their eyes met. Something reptilian slid across Smith's face before vanishing into its concealment. Gage's vision was fading.

He would get away with it. They wouldn't investigate. They'd leave it on the dead man. The simplest solution. And then, Smith would simply start again, carefully.

It's a piggyback, Gage thought incoherently. Sounds were growing indistinct. It's always a piggyback, someone else to take the blame. Like me.

"At least," he heard the Captain's voice, "it's over. Rest in peace, fucker."

The End

The Viruses of Quiet Desperation

The screaming starts as soon as he wakes up. It rises and falls hysterically, sporadically bubbling with terror. Sometimes it almost dies into a series of painful hacking gasps, but it always rises back to its desperate, bloody, tooth grinding peaks. Occasionally the wall thumped so hard the dishes rattled.

He lay there listening to it; eventually he gets up to brush his teeth. The phone begins to ring.

In the bathroom he faces the mirror as he brushes his teeth. It is a habit more than anything, the mirror is spray painted an uneven dull grey. He can hear the sound of the phone even over the screaming.

An image comes to him suddenly. He is standing in front of the mirror with a spray can, painting it.

He spits the last of the toothpaste into the sink. The screaming goes on and on, the phone is ringing insistently. He walks to the dingy kitchen and pours himself a glass of orange juice. He drinks it.

Eventually, he picks up the phone.

"I'm sorry," he says.

"It's all right," comes her voice. The screaming stopped.

"People owe things to each other," Jake tells him, the policeman's voice is controlled yet insistent, "just by being human beings. Once you touch someone, you can't walk away."

"There was nothing I could do," he insists, "nothing I could do for her. I'm sorry."

"Really, it's all right," she said.

They are in the hallway. He is standing by his door, embarrassed. She is on her knees, sopping up his vomit with pieces of Kleenex. She has a nervous smile, and a look to her that is lost and frightened. It wasn't an attractive look, he thinks, but rather a despairing one.

"No, I mean I hardly ever get sick like that. It's just that I was on a real bender last night."

He took a tentative step toward her.

"Don't worry about it. Sometimes things just get out of control."

She begins to slide the tissues into a paper bag. "I know about that," she finishes.

"Well, it's not fair that someone else has to clean up my messes. I feel bad enough as it is." He helps her with the last of the tissues. They stand up together.

"You look pretty bad," she says, "I have some herbal tea that might help, why don't you come inside."

Suddenly they are making love, his bare back heaves above her as her body stiffens intermittently. Her expression somewhere between pain and transcendence.

"First rule is you never fuck anyone who has more problems than you do," Jake is saying.

"For you that's an accomplishment." Jake is a police detective, he paces around the dingy apartment, fury caged by cracked fading paint and threadbare furniture.

He is in her living room. It's like a spiders nest, lines cross and criss-cross at every angle. Bizarre wire constructs and crystals hang suspended, like a cage from outside time and space. Light comes from strange directions. He is vaguely disoriented. She hands him a cup of herbal tea. The aroma is strange; it makes him think of the far east.

"The outer layers are a silver oxide paint. It's really expensive," she is saying, "the inner lattices are silver wire, and I keep them in place by laying duct tape over it. Silver is very strong.”

“What is it?” he asks, bewildered.

“It’s a sort of pentagram,” she explains, “like they use in magic for keeping demons in, or out. But in three dimensions.”

She laughs quietly; it is a broken little thing. “There are too many dimensions.”

He shivers then, and some part of him whispers to get up and leave her now. Whatever she’s involved in, wherever her head is from, he doesn’t want any part of it.

Instead, he looks down at the design at his feet.

“That’s my astrology chart,” she tells him, “I used it to see things. Shapes in the past and future.”

“It’s all wrong for an astrology chart,” he says. He’d seen them before, had dabbled in it, once long ago.

“No. Actually it’s the only working astrology chart in the world. You see astrology was invented by the Sumerians, and it was based on the positions of the stars then. But for the past six thousand years the stars have been drifting out of position. The old charts have been useless for almost two thousand years.”

At that moment, he can hardly bear to look at her, in the centre of her web of silver lunacy, but he does not leave. Where does he have to go, but to an empty dead apartment. At least she’s alive.

He is on his knees, the room is empty. He is bending over the chart with Kleenex in his hand. The chart is considerably faded, or maybe the light is just brighter. He traces a line with his fingertip. On and around the chart, shapes are outlined with chalk. The largest of them is the outline of a human leg. He touches it.

"It's completely accurate up to 2026," she says. She is sitting very close to him now, he is as conscious of her body, as of her words. Perhaps more.

"What about after 2026?" he asks her. His mouth feels very dry, his voice is rough.

"There is nothing after 2026. Nothing at all." She laughs nervously, the broken thing again. They are very close together. He touches her leg. She appears not to notice.

It's afterward. The sweat dries on their bodies, as they lay there.

"Thoughts are like viruses?" he asks, picking a thread from her soft monologue. He's been trying not to listen, but this has slipped through his defences.

"No. Thoughts are viruses," she corrects him, "they use us to transmit themselves. To reproduce themselves. Sometimes they take over and destroy their host."

"Are you saying they are alive?"

"I don't know. Is a virus alive? I think our whole history is just different breeds of viruses being transmitted farther and more efficiently with our exploration and our technology," she pauses. "It used to be we had to talk to each other, now we have television."

She seems so sad, when she says this. Sad and...his mind casts about for a word...obsolete.

She is outside his door. "They are coming closer. You have to let me in."

"What are they?" he almost asks, but realizes that he doesn't want to know.

He is sitting at his table, with a glass of orange juice. Her voice carries. The phone is ringing.

"They have doors, little doors everywhere. In 1940 they sealed the doors, but it only slowed them down. It didn't stop them. You must have seen the doors."

Outside the door she yells: "You have to let me in. There are things you have to know."

Inside he sits at his table. Behind him the television plays it makes no sound.

Jake turns off the television.

"What? You couldn't open a frigging door?" Jake swings back to him. "What the hell were you doing?"

Outside his apartment he drops his keys. The screaming goes on and on as he bends to retrieve them. He looks to his left.

"Do you remember the naughty beast?" she asks.

Jake shakes his head.

"It was a childhood monster that your parents tell you about. The thing was, it couldn't see you, if you couldn't see it. All you had to do to be safe was to close your eyes..."

"Yes," he says to her, there is something in her voice.

"I can't close my eyes," she whispers.

He looks up at Jake. "She said the doorways were opening. The dark lights were coming through."

"What the hell was that supposed to mean?" Jake asks, "What does that have to do with anything?"

"I'm seeing things now," he says to Jake. "I'm starting to see what's on the other side of the doors. Tentacles of dark light."

"Get a grip," Jake snarls "You're losing perspective."

As they lay together she swallows once and speaks. It has nothing to do with what they were talking about.

"Sometimes," she says "sometimes, I don't know if I'm remembering the future or looking into the past. Sometimes I get so lost in perspective that I can't find the now."

Disturbed, he kisses her. Her response comes from far away.

He is outside his apartment bent over his keys. Down the hall there is a shape, and a light.

She is outside his door. "You have to talk to me," she is saying.

"It was a mistake. I didn't want to get involved," he says to Jake.

"How can you not get involved?" Jake is yelling. "She was screaming right next door."

He lowers his head.

Abruptly the screaming starts. He jumps up, leaving his apartment, entering the hall. He races to her door. Just as he reaches for it there is a fierce thump and for a second it seems to bulge out towards him. A terrible light spills through the keyhole, and along the doorjambs. He backs away. Abruptly he is back in his apartment, locking the door and leaning against it.

The screaming goes on and on.

"Why did you paint the mirror?" Jake is asking. "Didn't you like what you saw?"

"If I can't see myself," he says, "maybe..." He does not finish the sentence. "Maybe they can't see me," is the unvoiced thought. He looks up suddenly.

The thing in the hallway is dark, and he can't quite make it out. It looks human, but the closer he looks the less human it is. Things like tentacles seem to twist and coil inside just below the surface. He picks up his keys.

"Do you think time is a particle or a wave?" she asks, "Most people see a wave; I think it's a particle."

"What's the difference?" he says. Her cup of herbal tea is cooling in his hands. He decides that he would like to kiss her.

"A wave is continuous," she explains, "it has a beginning and a middle and an ending. All in order."

"If it's a particle," she sits quite close to him, her teacup resting on her knees, "then every moment exists separate and indivisible from every other moment, each one forever."

He takes the teacup from her knee. She barely notices, lost in her vision of chaos.

"That every moment exists simultaneously, accessible from every other moment..." Chaos giving birth to strange order.

He kisses her.

The wall thumps hard and dishes rattle in the kitchenette. He reaches for the door...

The phone is ringing in his apartment. He picks it up.

"Help me," she says.

"You're dead," he speaks into the receiver, "I saw the body."

He is in her apartment now, kissing the chalk outlines, torn by need and pain. "I'm sorry," he whispers.

"Particles are accessible to each other," the answer comes through the phone line, "not just in the linear way we know. Particles speak to one another, see one another, particles can touch."

His mouth goes dry, and his heart pounds as he listens to the voice of the dead woman on the phone. Suddenly, he knows what she will say next.

"You can see them; do you know what that means?"

He hangs up abruptly. Particles touching, he thinks, backing away from the phone. Strange order.

"Viruses," Jake says, trying the word on, "There's more to it than that. Isn't there?"

"Yes," he tells Jake, "there are shapes." He closes his eyes. It won't help.

Inside, up against his door, he closes his eyes. The screaming goes on and on. He begins to scream.

"She screamed and she screamed and you didn't do anything." Jake is yelling at him. He doesn't say anything.

"You didn't even call for help," Jake yells.

They are laying together, the sweat drying on their bodies. "I love you," she says. He doesn't say anything.

"Am I under arrest?" he asks Jake.

Jake pauses, letting a silence stretch out. "No," he speaks finally, "but I want you to call me if anything else happens."

There is something beyond standard police work in Jake's voice, something almost caring. It strikes him, at that moment, that Jake is not just a police officer. Jake is human. Humans touch.

He is kneeling in the centre of the astrology pattern. Studying it. Behind him is a plastic police barricade. All around him are chalk outlines laid across her delicate traceries. Some of them are shaped like body parts. He bends down and kisses the outline that resembles a head.

He whispers to it, lips pressed against the outline, "I see it too."

"What did you see?" Jake is asking.

"I didn't see anything," he tells them.

"They can see you now," is what the voice on the phone would have said, if he hadn't hung it up. As he stares at it, the phone begins to ring again.

"What were all those lines and tapes?" Jake is asking him.

"Protection," she says.

"Concealment," she says.

"What was she afraid of?" Jake is asking.

"Viruses," he whispers.

"Viruses shape particles," she tells him as they lay together, "they make time linear, they impose cause and effect. But that's only one way to arrange time. There are other shapes, if you can see them, beyond the walls the viruses make for us."

She makes him feel claustrophobic. His body tenses.

"Don't leave me," she whispers.

"I hear her screaming all the time now. The particles are touching," he says.

"That's your guilt," Jake tells him.

"I'm starting to see it now," he says. "Shapes in the darkness, empty lights. I see the doors and the doorways. And I think it sees me."

"Listen to me:" Jake is saying. "She was insane. That's not your fault. She is dead. That's not really your fault either. You feel guilt. Your guilt is making you adopt her insanity."

There is an urgency in Jakes voice, as if intensity could fortify truth.

"If I can catch her insanity does that mean it's a virus? Does it destroy its host and reproduce itself, spreading like an infection?" He wonders. "Is it alive?"

Jake throws up his hands in frustration. "Come back to the human race," Jake snarls/pleads.

But Jake is drifting away.

He realizes with a flash of inspiration, as he watches Jake, inches away, but almost unimaginably distant, that he is losing human contact. Perhaps he has already lost it. Perhaps everyone is losing it. All those lives of lonely quiet desperation, of needing and fearing unbearably, they create a sort of vulnerability.

Vulnerability to what? He wonders.

To madness?

To viruses?

To the shapeless things waiting outside the walls of shaped linear time?

"It's safer on the inside," she tells him, just before they make love.

He doesn't understand, so he simply moans an almost word, as he revels in the feel of her.

He is on the inside now.

"I love you," he says into the phone. "I wasn't strong enough."

"I know," comes her voice over the phone.

"I need you," her voice. "Will you help me?"

"Yes," he says.

"Come to my place," her voice, "I need you."

"But there's nothing there anymore."

But he knows she's there, caught like a fly in amber. Trapped and suspended in a web outside time and space. Reaching out for human contact.

"I need you, will you come to me this time?"

Humanity means we need to touch each other, he thinks. What's left of us if we can't or won't?

He listens but the silence drags on, finally he says, "Yes."

He turns towards his door.

He is outside her door. He knows that whatever happens next, he has made his peace with the Gods of conscience. A terrible light spills from the keyhole and around the jambs. There is a roaring in his head.

He reaches for the doorknob.

The End

Silence

It was raining out, the wind roared and rain fell in sheets. It was night; the house was dark, except for a few upstairs lights.

There was a knock at the door.

There was no response, not even a dog barking.

Rapping sounded at the door again.

"Hello?" a voice called. "My van ran out of gas. I was wondering if I could use your phone?"

Nothing. Only silence from the empty rooms and still furniture, and the sound of wind and rain outside.

A few minutes passed.

There was the sound of scratching at the outside lock. Then nothing. A moment later, a window was pushed open. For a second, the house seemed to wait expectantly.

"Hello," called the figure, just outside the door. "Can I come in, the door's unlocked. I just want to use the phone."

Again, there was a still pregnant moment. A black canvas bag fell through the opened window. There was another ten seconds pause.

A figure crawled in. A woman.

The Thief was young, early twenties, wearing a leather and suede jacket and blue jeans. Her wet runners squeaked on the hardwood floor.

She lowered the window behind her, carefully not locking it.

There was a light switch beside the door. She flicked it. Lamplight flooded the room.

She was standing in the living room. There was a couch, large television, comfortable chairs. Bay windows opened onto it. The windows were one way. You couldn't see in. She'd discovered that.

"Hello?" she said. "Is anyone home? I just want to use the phone. My car broke down."

As she took off her soaking jacket and tied it to the canvas bag, her studied eye swept the room, cataloguing various items. Estimating their portability and value.

Off of the living room was a dining room. She walked in, looking around, taking in the heavy old wooden table. There was something solid and bulky about it. Its surface and edges looked scratched and scarred from long use. Probably an antique.

She stepped around, examining it. Along the edges of the table were deep runnels. She recognized it as part of an ancient grape press, the grape juice or wine, ran down the runnels.

The house smelled of money.

There were end tables up against the wall, a small door. She looked in. Just a closet of some sort.

In a corner of the dining room, near the closet, there was a dumbwaiter. She slid the door open and looked inside. Nothing. She slid the door shut and punched a button. UP. Only the barest whisper indicated that it worked.

She smiled, amused.

The Thief walked back to the hall, past the living room into the kitchen. She glanced around at the assortment of spotless kitchen gadgets. There was a heavy garbage disposal, an industrial sized blender.

There was a calendar on the kitchen door. She stared at it. Various dates were X'd out, including a three day period. The notation indicated airline times. She put her finger on the date. This was the second day of the trip.

Lots of time to empty the house.

On the other side of the kitchen were two doors. One lead to a pantry. From there, to the outdoors

She reached over to the phone hanging on the wall, fumbling in her pockets for the piece of paper with a phone number. She pressed buttons, paused, there was no dial tone.

The Thief listened for a moment. She flicked the receiver a few times. Still nothing. She stared at the receiver and hung up.

She poked around.

Climbing the stairs, she came to a bathroom. Sitting on the toilet, she used the bath towels to dry her hair. Getting up, she flushed and tossed the towels back onto the hooks. She examined the medicine cabinet, dropping a small assortment of drugs, Tylenol 3, Diazepam, Percocets, into her bag.

The Thief proceeded through the rooms, looking in drawers, and behind wall paintings. In the bedroom, she found a safe behind the medium sized painting of a clown. She left the painting crooked.

In the study, there was a larger floor safe. The Thief sat down at the desk, leaning back in the swivel chair. There was an opened package of cigarettes on the desk. She picked them up, shook one out, and put the rest in her pocket.

She opened the desk drawer and froze, the cigarette dangling from her lips.

There was a nickel plated pistol sitting in the desk drawer.

Gingerly, she reached out and picked it up, examining it carefully.

She pulled the trigger. A little flame appeared at the gunsight. She smiled and lit her cigarette.

The Thief pawed through the drawer, finding an assortment of papers and paraphernalia. There was a ring of keys. She set them carefully on the corner of the desk.

She pulled the drawer out completely and dumped it on the floor, examining the underside of the drawer. There was no combination written on the back of the drawer. She pulled another drawer out, and after rifling through it, emptied it and examined the back.

Two combinations.

The Thief smiled.

After emptying both safes, she skipped down the stairs into the living room.

The Thief picked up the remote and turned on the television. Sitting down in the comfortable lounge chair she put her feet up on the coffee table and channel surfed for a few minutes, pausing on the weather channel, before settling onto a Spanish language slasher film.

The light of the television cast strange shadows on her face as she watched it for a few minutes.

Abruptly, she got up and strode to the kitchen. Humming tunelessly, the television blaring softly in the other room, the Thief flung open the fridge door.

She grabbed a can of beer and popped the top, peering into the fridge. She sipped beer.

Pulling out a tub of margarine, she weighed it casually in her hands, before putting it on the counter. There was a jar of pickles, way back. Some cold meats. A couple of tomatoes in the bottom.

Lettuce? She wanted lettuce.

No lettuce in the crisper bottom tray.

There was a salad bowl, covered with tinfoil.

Any old port in a storm.

She pulled it forward to the edge of the fridge and peeled back the tinfoil.

In the bowl, smothered in lettuce, was a severed human head.

Beer went spraying out of her mouth as she pinwheeled backwards. The bowl, overbalanced tipped off its ledge and tumbled out of the fridge, lettuce flying everywhere. She watched with wide eyes, mouth gaping, coughing as the head rolled across the floor, coming to rest on its cheek, staring at nothing at all.

The can of beer lay beside her, gulping as it emptied its contents. Quickly, she set it upright.

The Thief sat there on the floor for a few minutes, staring.

The mouth hung wide open, smeared with garish lipstick, unseeing eyes thick with mascara. It was a woman's head, but the makeup had been inexpertly applied. Probably after death.

As if galvanized, she scrambled across the floor, tossing lettuce back in the bowl. Her features twisted as she used the tinfoil to grab the head and replace it. She covered the salad bowl with the tinfoil as best she could, and shoved it back into the refrigerator.

The Thief held the refrigerator shut, as if afraid it would open on its own, and took three deep breaths.

She looked around wildly, then hurriedly stuffed the condiments back into the fridge.

The beer went into the trash. Hurriedly, she used dish towels to wipe up the spilled beer, squeezing them out, running them under the sink and mopping up some more. She stuffed the soggy towels into a small garbage bag, and then shoved them into the bottom tray of the fridge.

Striding back into the living room, she shut off the television.

A sudden wash of light flooded the living room. The Thief ran to the door window.

A car was pulling in, she couldn't see more than the glare of its lights.

She retreated back into the room for a second, chewing on her lip.

Outside, in the rain, she thought she heard the sound of a car door opening and closing. She looked around wildly.

The lights were on all over the house.

There was a scuff mark on the shimmering coffee table where she'd put her foot up. She moved an ash tray to cover it.

Grabbing her bag, she headed back to the kitchen, running swiftly to the pantry door.

Locked. Double locked, inside and out. You'd need a key to open it from the inside as well.

The Thief stepped back into the kitchen, her eyes darted. The loaf of bread she'd taken was still out, butter knife beside it. She grabbed the loaf and tucked it under her arm, holding the butter knife like a weapon.

The front door creaked open. She looked up.

The door closed.

She had to retreat. The Thief opened the other door; it was a shallow closet full of brooms. The next one led to a staircase that yawned into absolute darkness.

She closed the door gently behind her, standing just inside, listening.

Footsteps padded into the kitchen.

Moving cautiously, she retreated down the steps.

A step creaked loudly. Heart pounding, she stopped, a cold sweat breaking out over her body. There was no reaction. Then she continued, carefully as she could.

She took a few tentative steps into the darkness, reaching into her pocket for matches.

Suddenly the basement lights turned on. She heard heavy footsteps on the stairs.

Taking in the basement at a glance she saw an assembly of crates and trunks, rough hewn wooden walls, locked by simple doors. The basement had been sectioned off; the area that she was in was small. She'd hoped to hide behind the furnace, but it was behind one of the locked doors.

Who would lock the doors in the basement?

The sort of man who would keep a severed human head in the refrigerator.

The Thief crouched behind the stairs, turning her face away into the wall. The stair creaked loudly above her. She struggled not to whimper, her body trembled uncontrollably. Three more footsteps. A shadow passed over her, footsteps moving past. Keys rattled. There was the sound of a lock being turned.

She looked out to see a broad back disappearing into one of the rooms.

The Thief stuffed the loaf of bread under the stair. Scrambling out from behind the stairs she began to climb the steps. On the third step, her foot hovering above the next step, she stopped. Brow furrowing with concentration, the Thief slowly lowered her foot to the fourth step and leaned weight on it.

Nothing.

With a sigh of relief, she lifted her foot high, skipping the next step and pulled herself up. Moving as quietly as she could, she fled up the next few steps out into the kitchen.

For a second, the Thief examined the basement door, but could see no effective way to lock it. Down there, she could hear the man moving around.

She walked quickly and carefully through the kitchen, into the hallway, moving down until she was at the door. She didn't see anyone else. She grabbed the doorknob.

It was locked. She grimaced. Double lock. You'd need a key to get in or out. It was a security measure that was becoming increasingly common to prevent burglars from simply breaking a window and reaching in to unlock the door.

She stepped over to the window she had come through, and tried to gently pull it open. It came up a few inches with an audible creak. She put down her bag and pulled harder, it resisted.

Behind her, with senses made acute by fear, she heard the basement door open in the kitchen. Unconcerned footsteps began moving towards her.

She turned around and around in a slow circle. Then she leaped up the stairs, taking them two at a time. At the top of the stairs she halted. She'd forgotten her bag. She turned and descended a few steps, retreating suddenly, as a shape passed beneath.

The Thief waited, her heart pounding. She listened.

The footsteps moved on. The dining room door opened, but she didn't hear it close.

She crept halfway down the stairs. She could see the curtains fluttering in the breeze of the open window, and her black bag sitting in the corner. Just out of sight, she could hear the man moving around.

She listened for a moment, creeping further until she was almost at the base of the stairs. Staring at the bag, the Thief listened to the sounds of movement.

She squinted and licked her lips.

Then quickly, gracefully, she took three steps out into the hall, grabbed the bag, and withdrew back up the stairs.

She froze, the movements in the dining room had stopped. Holding her breath, she waited. Abruptly, the figure crossed her line of view, stepping to the window. It creaked as the man pushed it shut. The figure pushed the curtains aside, staring out the window for a second.

At the figure's feet, she could see a small puddle of water and droplets where the rain had seeped in through the evening. She stared at his wet footprints glistening, leading away towards the stairs. Her stomach fluttered, and her heart started to pound against her ribs.

The figure turned and without hesitation, walked back the way it came.

She let her breath out, exhaling softly, trembling with relief.

Listening carefully to the sounds of movement downstairs, she proceeded quietly into the study, closing the bedroom door as she passed it.

Kneeling beside the desk, she grabbed the keys from the desk corner. The Thief stared helplessly at the elaborate key ring, at its dozen keys. The nickel plated lighter/pistol was there beside them. On impulse, she snatched it.

There was the soft creak of footsteps on the stair.

She looked up, panicked, and began to fumble objects back into the drawers. She pushed them back in, one at a time.

The bedroom! She remembered the state she had left it in. She wanted to rush into the bedroom and shove the drawers shut. To close the wall safe, spinning the dial to lock it and put the picture of the clown back over it. She could hide in the closet, or under the bed.

The safe.

She glanced across the study. The floor safe's door hung open.

The footsteps had reached the top of the stairs.

The footsteps were coming towards her. The Thief closed the safe door, but it would take a yank on the handle and a spin of the dial to lock it. There wasn't time.

The footsteps were almost at the study. She took one last look around to see if anything was missing.

The Thief ducked under the desk, hiding.

Suddenly, she felt the cigarettes in her pocket. Squirming, she threw the package of cigarettes onto the desk.

The door swung open.

Sweating, breath caught in her throat, heart pounding, she listened as the footsteps approached, heading straight towards her.

They stopped. She heard rustling sounds above her. The cigarettes. The Thief listened as the man took a cigarette out of the pack, slipped the package into his pocket.

The man walked around the desk. She could see his legs, inches from her.

The man pulled the desk drawer open and began rifling through it. Underneath, she watched the man's legs. The man was looking for the cigarette lighter, she realized. She clutched it in her hands and whispered a silent prayer.

The man opened another drawer and shuffled through papers.

Abruptly, the figure got up from the desk and walked away, into the bedroom. Under the desk, the Thief could hear a drawer opening, the sound of a match being struck.

She heard the man exhale.

More footsteps. The Thief bent down, pressing her face to the floor so she could peek out from under the desk. She caught a glimpse of the man's feet down the hall.

Heading for the bathroom.

The Thief's blood ran cold. Had she remembered to flush? She hadn't cared. She'd used the towels. In her mind's eye, she saw them, hanging in disarray. She visualized the man starring at them, in growing recognition of her presence.

She heard the sound of a thin stream of urine striking the bowl.

The Thief scrambled out from under the desk, heading for the hall. The floor creaked loudly under her. She slammed to a stop.

The sound of urination stopped. She held her breath, standing in the hallway. The bathroom door was open. She could almost see the man's shadow spilling out of it. She waited.

The sound of urination started up again.

The Thief backed away in barely controlled panic.

Up against the wall, there was a dumbwaiter. She sidled over to it, until the bathroom door was out of sight around the corner. A little metal plaque announced it was rated for 200 pounds. Another note indicated unsafe for human use.

The Thief slid open the dumbwaiter door. There was enough room, she crawled in, pressed the button, and slid the door shut.

The dumbwaiter silently slid down to the main floor. Sliding open the door, she froze.

She was staring at a nude woman lying on the dining room table.

The woman's head turned. She stared at the Thief. She had blue eyes.

She was gagged, the Thief realized after a heartbeat. She was spread eagled on the table, her wrists and ankles bound tightly around with cords anchoring her to the legs underneath.

The Thief put her finger to her lips as she climbed out.

The woman's eyes were pleading, her jaw worked.

The Thief smiled and shrugged apologetically, sidling around the table past the woman. She moved her head to follow the Thief, blinking.

At the base of the table was a five gallon plastic bucket. It was to collect the blood, the Thief realized. The blood would spill down the runnels around the table, and into the buckets.

The woman squeaked through the gag.

From the base of the table, the Thief looked up at her, past bruises on her legs, past her black pubic thatch, exposed immodestly, past her breasts, the nipples hardened by fear, to her raised head, her pleading eyes. She squeaked again.

The toilet flushed.

They both glanced up at the ceiling.

The Thief spread her hands helplessly, and grinned at the woman. She mouthed silent words of reassurance and then turned her back. Water ran in the sink upstairs.

She stepped into the hall, looking for a likely window. Not the one she'd come through, that had made too much noise. She put down her bag and jerked the window up with all her might. It came with barely a squeak.

The Thief looked back to where the bound woman was.

She stared back out the open window into the safe and welcoming darkness.

She turned quickly, and rushed back into the room. The Thief brushed her hand against the woman's hair, her teeth bared in something that wasn't quite reassurance, and placed the lighter/pistol on a dresser beside the table, up against the wall.

She worked at the binding around the woman's left wrist. She pulled. It came free. They heard steps descending the stairs. The Thief left off as the woman reached over, pulling desperately at her other wrist's bonds.

The Thief scanned the room wildly. There was the small service alcove, the closet just off the dumbwaiter, she stepped into it, pulling the door half closed.

She heard the door into the dining room swing open; saw the woman freeze, staring in horror. The woman uttered a muffled shriek around her gag.

The Thief pressed herself as far back into the service closet as she could, sinking to her knees, trembling as she watched the flurry of motion through the crack in the door. The sound of flesh slapping against flesh rang out.

Had he hit her? Had she lashed out? Had he slammed her head against the table?

The struggle ceased abruptly.

For a second, there was no sound, except tortured breathing. She tried to muffle her own, to breathe slowly and calmly, but each breath she took seemed to push her harder, until she was almost hyperventilating. The sure knowledge that he must hear her almost tore a scream out of her. She stuffed the corner of her jacket into his mouth, biting on it, breathing through her nose.

She saw the pistol/lighter glinting on the table. It seemed monstrously huge. Any moment now, he'd look at it. He'd see it, and know there was someone else in the house.

The man, without apparently looking, placed a pistol on the table beside it, further up. A real gun. It appeared identical to the lighter.

On trembling knees, the Thief straightened up. Staring through the break in the door, she could see the man undressing. His back was to the Thief's closet.

As quietly as she could, the Thief stepped forward the two or three feet to the table and retrieved the gun.

A second later, the man turned and picked up the lighter/pistol.

The Thief clutched the gun to her breasts, squeezing the handle.

Through the crack in the door, she watched the man caressing the bound woman with the lighter. The woman jerked, as he drew it along the curve of her leg. Her hips lifted as the barrel probed through her pubic hair. The false weapon slid up her stomach, circled her breasts.

The woman turned her face away, whimpering through the gag, as he slid the barrel against her cheek. The Thief watched the man seize the woman's head, holding it steady by force. She struggled, her whole body thrashing against the ropes that bound it tightly.

The Thief took a deep breath and held the gun out in front of her. She steeled herself to rush out.

Did the gun have a safety? Was it on? She paused and ran her free hand over the gun, feeling strange metal ridges and protrusions.

Her fingers felt a rectangular hole in the bottom of the gun. She turned the weapon over and stared at the hole in mute uncomprehending shock.

From the table there was a sudden click, a sharp odour of urine assaulted her nostrils. She looked out through the crack in the door. She'd opened the door wider retrieving the useless weapon. Now she was afraid to close it further, fearing the movement would attract his attention.

The lighter was pressed against the woman's temple, its flame on. The Thief could see the man now; see a fleeting expression of surprise as he stared at the lighter flame. The pistol clip hung loosely clenched in his other hand.

He'd meant to fire the empty pistol, the Thief realized, and then show her the clip.

The woman's eyes were wet with tears.

The man could have made a mistake, the Thief thought desperately. He might think he'd accidentally left the pistol/lighter in the dining room, and picked up the wrong weapon by mistake.

But he knew where he'd put the pistol.

What happened when he looked back for it, and it wasn't there?

He would know.

The woman screeched around the gag, struggled wildly. The man grabbed her. Again, for a second, his back was to the door.

The Thief put the useless weapon back on the table, almost hidden beside a book.

The man turned and picked it up. There was a click, as of the clip being shoved back into place. The Thief watched through the crack, the man put placed gun and the lighter on another narrow wall table behind the woman.

With economical movements, he removed the other objects, books, magazines, a small vase of flowers, from the table near the Thief to the other table.

The man stood at the table. The Thief shrunk back, crouching. She could see the man's arms; almost see the tip of his face in profile as the man unrolled a leather packet. The man lifted it. The Thief caught glints of silver. Silver and surgical sharpness.

The man laid it standing upright against the edge of the table. With professional calm, the man unrolled another leather bundle, pushing it against the first, so that it held the first in its upright position.

With exquisite care the man began unwrapping separate, strange silver instruments. They caught the light as he held them, exposing strange curves and clasps and serrated sharp edges.

Through the crack in the door, the Thief could see the woman glancing at the man, then determinedly looking away.

The man turned to the woman.

He caressed her forehead. Tried to pull her face over to look at the instruments. She struggled. He gripped her head fiercely, turning it to face the rows of instruments. Reaching into her eyes with his fingers, he pulled her eyelids open, holding her so she could stare.

The Thief stuffed the corner of her jacket into her mouth, breathing hard. Her stomach churned, a pit of acid. She struggled not to throw up.

Abruptly, the man released the woman, heading towards the closet.

The Thief almost screamed.

But the man just stood in front of the table. The Thief watched the man's hand gently touch the instruments, fingering their surfaces in mock indecision.

The Thief could see the gun on the table behind the woman's head. She would have to get past the man to reach it.

The hand selected a delicate scalpel and withdrew.

The Thief stared at the glints of silver and almost reached for them. It would at least make them almost equal.

No. The man was too close to the gun.

Through the crack, she saw the man caressing the woman's face with the scalpel. His face close against hers, he slid the scalpel down between her breasts, sighting along the line of her body.

Past her body. The Thief watched the man's expression shift as he stared down past the line of her body, out the dining room.

He'd seen something.

The man stood up from the bound woman, staring out of the room. The Thief shrunk back further into the closet, pressing herself against the wall, staring hypnotized at the crack, and at the slice of the man it revealed.

Suddenly, it moved. The man crossed in front of the table, stepping out of the room.

The Thief waited a heartbeat. She left the closet, stepping towards the gun. She grabbed the longest knife she could see from the leather casings. Four strides took her to the pistol. Her hand hovered uncertainly. The pistol and the lighter were identical.

Behind her, the woman squeaked.

She turned.

The man was standing there, on the other side of the table, naked, holding her black bag. He was huge, well over six feet tall; his frame was ridged with muscles. The man grinned, baring perfect teeth, his blue eyes flashing.

He rushed the Thief. The black bag bounced off the Thief's body as she grabbed for the gun. The man was almost on top of her. She waved the knife and pulled the trigger. A small flame appeared at the end of the pistol muzzle.

The man slammed her up against the wall, the lighter flying from her hand. The table overturned. The Thief, struggling wildly somehow pushed the man back. They fell against the dining table, for a brief second, the Thief felt the woman's body at her back. Then they rolled off.

The Thief came down on top of the man. Her knee kicked, but missed the man's groin. He held her wrist in a vicelike grip, forcing the knife from her nerveless fingers. The man, grinning, punched the Thief. They rolled until the man was on top of the Thief. He slammed the Thief's head against the floor. Blood filled her nostrils.

Out of the corner of her eye, the Thief saw a glint of nickel plated silver. With a final effort, she squirmed out from under the man and scrambled across the floor towards it.

As her fingers closed on it, she froze at the touch of something small and hard at the base of her skull.

Carefully, she turned, looking back.

The man, grinning, held the pistol above the Thief's eyes, pressing against her forehead.

His blue eyes flashed, his grin grew even wider, his pearl white teeth gleamed.

He pulled the trigger.

A small lighter flame emerged.

* * *

It was raining out. Thunder pealed and lightning cracked, rain came down in sheets.

The door to the house opened, its white silhouette of interior light cutting through the night.

What Devours Also Hungers – Page 63

The Thief stepped out into the rain, ignoring it, glancing around. Behind her, came the woman, dressed now.

Calmly, they walked to the car. The Thief selected among keys until he found one that opened the car door. The woman entered the car, reaching over to unlock the other door as the Thief crossed over.

After a moment, the car started up and drove away.

The rain continued to pour.

The End

Write Me

Jerome had supper waiting by the time his five year old son, Matthew, arrived home from work.

"What's on?" asked Matthew as he stepped into the tiny apartment. The light pseudo-gravity gave his steps an incongruously youthful bounce.

"Algae base B and D with beef culture, prepared in neo-French mode," Jerome replied, he enjoyed cooking.

Sadly, Matthew seemed to have no particular interest in it.

Hilary had loved his cooking. But Hilary was long gone. Sometimes, Jerome found himself wishing she hadn't left. But she had, and all he was left with was the pain of her memory.

But at least, he thought, it was real memory.

Jerome watched in silence as Matthew shed his work devices, carefully locking them into separate cases.

Then he moved around the apartment, performing minor straightenings. Matthew was meticulous.

When he finished, he sat at the table and began to eat. After a moment, Jerome joined him.

"So," Jerome asked, "how was your day?"

"A waste of time," replied Matthew, speaking between measured bites, "we had a series of pipelines up from Earth, but the data was hopelessly corrupted. We couldn't do anything with it, so in the end, we had to requisition new beams."

"Oh."

"The comptrollers were mad as hell. It seems they had a budget line for data reconstruction, but their allocation for replacement feeds was used up. It took us most of the day to convince them that we couldn't fix this load and that they'd have to find the money somehow."

"Uh huh."

"Bureaucrats." Matthew made a face.

Jerome picked at his food, watching Matthew eat with indifferent haste. Food didn't matter to Matthew. He took time out to consume, and then moved on.

"I thought it would be good for us to eat together," Jerome said, "you know. With the way our schedules conflict, we don't really see much of each other sometimes. And you're still a juvenile, there are regs..."

"Yes, I've been studying them. Did you know that between twelve and seventeen I'll have fewer rights than I do now? Something to do with hormonal development at that stage. Isn't that insane?"

"I guess so," Jerome replied. He watched the old man in his son's young body.

"What I find that I notice now, though, are the gaps."

"Gaps?" Jerome asked.

"Developmental stages," Matthew explained, "in the old days children would go through a series of developmental stages, where perceptions and reasoning abilities were different in kind and in quality from one level to another. Such as making sense of three-D and two-D images."

"I didn't think that would bother you."

"The stages, the built in limitations, are partly biological, partly the wiring development of the physical structure of the brain. They're still there. With writing, you can build bridges over them. But every now and then, you find a gap filled in beyond the software bridge. That's when you realize it was there. You discover that you have broader insights."

"Oh," said Jerome.

"I've talked to others in my age group, it's a common experience."

"They said your personality would evolve," Jerome offered. From day one, they had told him, Matthew would evolve, until ultimately, he would be, more or less, who he would have been anyway.

They lied; Jerome thought bitterly, nobody could know that.

"Who?" Matthew asked.

"The Overwriters," Jerome replied.

The conversation staggered to a halt for a few moments. They ate quietly.

"I was reading this article," Jerome ventured, "about new advances in writing. It seems they're having some success writing partial programs on criminals."

A criminal, Jerome reflected angrily, was anyone considered to be socially maladapted and therefore subject to reduced civil rights in comparison to their age and social group. Incorrigibles were liable to be dumped and written over. So were suicides, but suicides would not be amenable to partial writes.

"It's not my field, but I doubt it," Matthew replied, "you can't avoid overwriting. It's like a computer program saved on a matrix. It's holographic, it won't work with a piece missing here and a piece missing there. If you write a new program onto the matrix, and it doesn't identify the old one, it'll write itself over parts of the old program, and then you have junk."

"That's why," he looked up, "sometimes when you lose a file in your computer system, you can sometimes get it back. The computer hasn't erased it; it's just 'forgotten' to recognize it. You can get it back, by having the computer recognize it again."

"That's also why, if you want it back, you can't enter anything else until you have it. If the computer doesn't recognize the program, it'll write over it as if it wasn't there," Matthew concluded, "and then it's destroyed."

"So all they have to do is learn to recognize the human coding..." Jerome speculated.

"Human coding is wired differently, its whole brain organization. Global or integrated; not modular like computers. There's no way to avoid overwriting."

"But they have had some successes," Jerome insisted.

"As I understand it," replied Matthew drawing on professional expertise, "they've been trying to overwrite so as to limit the damage. They still wind up with badly dysfunctioning personalities."

"But," Matthew continued, "I'd say the biggest obstacle is in the complete incompatibility of the original and new programs. They simply don't integrate."

"Oh," said Jerome.

Jerome stopped eating, and simply watched Matthew.

He looked like Hilary, Jerome decided for the thousandth time. He had her eyes, and traces of her face. Perhaps it was guilt that made him think that. It seemed that nothing else of theirs was in the boy.

"Matthew?"

The child stopped and looked up, grave eyes measuring, "What?"

"Do you ever miss it?"

"Miss what?"

"Being a real child?"

"I am a real child. I've certainly got enough restrictions on my civil rights."

"You know what I mean. Does it ever bother you, having a written personality? Are you missing something?

Jerome suddenly flashed back to the Writingday, as it had come to be called. He and Hilary had taken the grinning burbling toddler into the center. Had watched as the technicians took him away. When Matthew returned, Hilary had been gone. A technician had introduced him to his son.

The two of them had formally shaken hands.

"You mean do I miss squalling and bedwetting? Do I feel somehow deprived in losing the opportunity to go stumbling along at a snail's pace, being immature unformed clay, a grasping well of helpless needs, a half person living a mock life?" Matthew asked rhetorically.

"No, I don't think so," he concluded.

"Besides," Matthew started again, "this isn't Earth, where oxygen is free and water falls from the sky. Everything has a cost here, even breathing. We simply can't afford to coddle our members for twenty-five years until they become mature adults and learn useful skills. Members of our society have to pull their own weight as soon as possible."

The party line, thought Jerome, they wrote the party line into him.

"I want a divorce."

Jerome said it softly but clearly.

There was a moment of tense and arching silence, Matthew simply looked at him.

"As a legal juvenile, I have primary rights to the family domicile," he said.

"I know," Jerome answered, "I've found alternate accommodations."

"You're leaving." The child's lip began to tremble. Jerome felt a stabbing pain in his heart, but steeled himself against the sensation. A trick of the writing, he told himself.

"Yes. There really is no point in going on," Jerome said.

"Why?" Matthew asked, almost plaintively.

"You're not my son," Jerome explained.

"I am! I am too your son!" Matthew burst out.

Beneath the table he wrung his tiny hands together. It was an old man's gesture, not a child's. There was nothing of the child in Matthew, it seemed to Jerome.

"My son is gone; you're just a generic personality that's replaced him. You're a ghost from the machines, and someone else's ghost as well."

You couldn't electronically insert information into the human mind without damaging it. The obvious solution had been to destroy the mind, erase it completely, and insert a new personality along with the information.

So brutally, callously obvious, thought Jerome.

Matthew had been gone. Whoever, whatever Matthew might have become had been gone since the technician had stepped through the door with him.

Jerome suddenly experienced a flush of relief, he felt free. Freed from pretending, free to grieve for his lost son, free from the cautious dance with this stranger.

You'll grow to love him, they said, and he'll love you. The divorce rates exposed that lie. Bonds in that unforgiving land of family and strangers, he realized, eventually became unbearable.

"Write yourself," Matthew snapped angrily. "You made me this way. You decided to write me. It wasn't my choice. You and Mom could have chosen not to."

Guilt stabbed at Jerome. It was the first time he'd ever heard Matthew refer to Hilary.

She'd wanted to waive overwriting.

But Jerome hadn't agreed. They couldn't afford the lifetime taxes, and fees, and surcharges, he'd told her. Besides, he'd said, no one else did it anymore. He'd not had the courage to buck the wave of social pressure, or suffer the penalties.

"I don't think that this is helping," he told Matthew. "I'm going now. Under the regulations you can have the next four days to yourself, or you can call Family Services and requisition an interim parent."

Jerome got up and walked to the Portal. He didn't bother looking around the sterile grey quarters. Nothing here felt like it was his.

"Don't go," Matthew called.

Jerome hesitated. He turned back at the portal, as it slid open.

"You can start interviewing replacement parentals...I think...it would be better with someone who didn't know you from before."

He looked down.

"I'll keep in touch."

Then he was gone, the portal swished shut quietly to mark his absence.

Matthew sat alone at the table. He stared at his small hands, watching them curl into fists again and again.

"Write me," he whispered.

The End

Moonwalker

"It was a new world out there, a merciless inhuman world. The only way to deal with it was to run or die...or change," ancient corroded words.

Lacey turned the pages of the antique fetish magazine; the flesh of her arms now the colour and texture of rotting bananas.

Behind her, on the wall screen, images of penguins and dolphins, ragged wretched looking creatures, were interspersed with scenes of viscous waters and the great seeder ships futilely pumping out their millions of tons of genetically enhanced algae and plankton.

An earnest, harried young man's face filled the screen.

"This is it," he said, "the last big chance, if we lose the Pacific, we might as well give up and go to the moon."

She ignored it.

They weren't going to save the Pacific Ocean.

The images in the magazine, sleek inhuman bodies in shimmering leather and latex, contorted in agony or ecstasy fascinated her.

It was like they knew, she thought. They knew that the world was going to change, and that there would be new paradigms, new beauty. Hard and leathery, slick and glossy, featureless textures, and metal studs, an extreme inhuman fashion was being born.

There was a dull roar in her apartment and the walls shook. Outside a PostHarrier Squad car directed a cushion of pressurized air against her building to make a turn. As it rolled outside her window, she caught a glimpse of its underbelly, studded with thumpers, jetters and laydowns.

Lacey had seen men torn apart by thumpers alone.

Jerold gurgled in the bathroom. She ignored him.

She walked to the window, edging around curling growths, but by the time she got there, the PostHarrier was just disappearing around the corner, careening from building to building, bouncing on its invisible cushions.

The corner of her window display: Oxygen content, down to sixteen per cent, birds would be dying in flight again. A list of toxic constituents in the atmosphere, and in the rain. Ultraviolet and radiation indexes.

She barely registered it.

She stood beside the window, staring out into the ruined, dilapidated streets, and perpetual toxic rains. Not even weeds grew anymore. The street below roiled; a sea of derelict and desperate lives, human rats, predators. No matter how you tried to keep them out, they got in.

Six months ago, Lacey had been gang raped in a secured parking lot.

Even beyond the horror of what they did to her, she remembered the insectile unblinking security cameras turn to watch her. To relentlessly record her torment. Nobody had come. Whoever it had been behind that unblinking lens had simply watched.

Perhaps there had been no one watching at all, just banks of empty television screens glowing softly in some room somewhere. Perhaps not even that, digital video feeds reduced to ones and zeros, stored on endless rows of massive storage crystals. A mindless digital god, endlessly recording, seeing everything and caring about nothing.

In the end, her rape simply wasn't important. Not to the rapists, who'd forgotten her moments after finishing. Not to the watchers. Not even, she had realized, to herself. Things were so much worse, so claustrophobically awful, that it was simply trivial.

There was no safe place, anymore.

* * *

Lacey woke up. There was a storm outside. She could hear the distant crack of thunder, the pounding of rain and wind. The rotting luminosity of the city poured faint light through her bedroom window.

Sheets of water, thick and textured with oils and soots, rolled down the outside of transparent cellular plastic. Real glass could no longer survive out there.

Idly, she watched a bug crawling along the inside of her window. She reached out, plucked it, popped it into her mouth, and chewed slowly. She'd had strange appetites of late.

Her skin was now completely black. Not a human black, not shades of melanin, rather the soft black of bananas gone completely rotten. It tore easily, whenever she moved, viscous, translucent oil spilling out. But there was no pain when her skin tore, more and more she simply ignored it. The apartment was full of stains from the oils that seeped from the rents in her skin.

Intrigued by thoughts of appetite, she went to her computer, ignoring the glossy pages and the glossy models of the magazine. A wiry moss was growing over it, but she kept the screen and the keyboard clear. There were a series of inquiries dating back weeks from her work, along with fresher, increasingly urgent queries from creditors. She fed them enough data and enough funds to make them leave her alone. She estimated that she had two months, before her finances became untenable.

She studied the list of nannomorphing proteins, rewriting flesh and blood into intricate carbon lattices. Yes. She had stolen all the supplements that she would need from work.

Idly she played with her antique coins, nickels and quarters, bending them flat between thumb and forefinger.

Now the wall screen began to talk about the new domed cities being built on the moon.

They didn't talk about the slave labour though. They didn't talk about the Xenomorphic Viral complexes used to transform human beings into things that could exist naked on the surface, the Moonwalkers. About the careful ecology that had been designed for those inhuman conditions. Designed to eventually wither and die.

Lacey had helped to design the Moonwalkers.

It was a very simple concept. To colonize an alien world, design people that could live there. At least until you'd made things ready for the normal people, the elites wealthy enough to abandon this rotting dying world for one of domed cities and purified air. Then the Moonwalkers would die off, expiration coded into their new genetic profiles. Like the cast offs on Earth, they would have served their purpose.

The new future belonged to the Elites, the ones who would cast off the withered husk of Earth, to chart humanity's future. The next chapter in the human adventure would be theirs, going boldly forth, leaving the rest behind, forgotten. After all, they couldn't live here anymore.

No one could.

Earth was becoming inimical to human life.

. Somehow, the human race had become invitation only, as far as those who'd been excluded by the Elites were concerned.

The people who decided who mattered, decided the future was somewhere else. They planned to ruin the old world to build the new, the way ancient Alexandria had been broken down to supply the stone to build Cairo. The new devours the old, builds palaces on ancient bones.

After she'd been raped, she'd crawled back to her apartment, blacked the window and turned off the wall screen. She'd curled up in her mother's old blanket, trying to shut the world out.

Instead, there in the darkness, she'd heard it. The screaming rumbles of PostHarriers, police cars and ambulances. The soft moans of the wind, the creaks and whines of the building itself, the way it hummed, the rasp of the filtration systems.

Last year the filtration had failed and nineteen people had died in their sleep. The families of the survivors had foregone lawsuits in exchange for first priority to the vacated apartments.

This was a tomb, she'd thought then.

* * *

It was getting harder to move.

Lacey examined Jerrold in the bathroom. He was no longer recognizable, she thought. The last vestiges of human form had been colonized away. The bathroom was overrun with a complex of glistening tubes and webbings, of inscrutable pumping purple organs.

Idly she broke off a tube and put it in her mouth, sucking on it, swallowing her own teeth for the calcium. Her jaw was almost fused.

Her apartment was getting crowded. She would have to make more room, while she was still able to.

There was old Miss McLandress in the apartment beyond this wall. An old woman without family or visitors, sitting at the window like she did, watching the world die by inches.

Lacey didn't want to do it.

She liked Ms McLandress.

What Devours Also Hungers – Page 77

But then again... She was old and withered; just waiting to die really.....

The way Lacey had waited to die.

Lacey reached out and crumbled the wall between them, the weakened masonry turning to dust under her claws. She stepped through.

Miss McLandress didn't struggle at all.

* * *

Lacey admired herself in the mirror. Her hard body glistening black armour, a fetish insect dream of curves and angles, face a featureless dark mirror, vents and feeder tubes and valves studding her abdomen in wonderful symmetry. Something new and pure.

Something without an expiration built into her genes this time.

She was now something that could live in this world or any other. That could explore the Marianas Trench, stroll on Mount Everest, or walk the surface of the moon. Free of fear, free from the human maggots that swarmed the decaying body of the world.

Her apartment contained an entire ecology emerging, contained, waiting to unfold, waiting to bloom. A vibrant, violent, shimmering ecology, life of smoot surfaces and armour. A glistening future, struggling from the broken husk of the old world.

They would be gone soon. It was no longer a world for human beings. Now, she felt a modicum of sympathy for them and their desperate mindless savagery. To her, they were no longer human. The paradigm of what was human had shifted.

Perhaps, as the magazines hinted, it had slowly been shifting for a long time. Humanity unconsciously realizing what it had to become. Yearning blind and inchoate.

They were dying.

What Devours Also Hungers – Page 78

What they were was dying.

For them, the whole world was a tomb.

No wonder they were so desperate to escape, to do terrible things to each other for a moment's pleasure, to enslave and dehumanize each other so they could feel human.

Except for the apartment. This was a womb. The future was being born here. The real future, not the tediously recycled self-indulgences of sterile Elites gazing into endless mirrors. They had merely chosen a different kind of death.

It was time for something new. Time for something to be born that could live in this world that the rest of humanity had made for her.

Lacey walked out into the world.

The End

The First Men

"Before you were Men, before you walked on two legs and looked up at the sky, before you dreamt and made things, before your first village and long before you filled the world with cities... we were Men, we were all that you are now, and more, greater. And now, what we have become... in time, you will be like us... Ghouls"

***

Three million years ago. On the African Savannah a troop of monkeys, baboons, huddle together on the plains, watching a pride of lions at their kill. Science will call them Theropithecus Ungulata.

Theropithecus Ungulata is large for a monkey, large even for a baboon. The males stand 1.8 meters tall, weigh in at 65 kilograms. But this is the era of primates, and the Theropithecus lineage has flowered. Theropithecus Oswaldi, and Dinopithecus, also Baboons for instance are larger.

But Theropithecus Ungulata is unique. It has perfectly adapted to the open savannah, to live without shelter. Ungulata has learned to run with the gazelles and the antelope; it has adopted a semi-bipedal stance, and a loping running gait that eats up the miles. Ungulata runs on its toes, formerly a semi-grasping paw, five digits have been reduced to two, forming a cloven pseudo-hoof. A necessity for ceaseless movement, perpetual running.

But there are other distances, behind that baboon muzzle, those canines, that ironic fixed grin, Theropithecus Ungulata looks out at the world with a through focused eyes and heavy brow, and a brain case of 1300 cubic centimeters.

The rough forepaws, freed from much of the burden of locomotion are highly dextrous and powerful. In the impoverished environment of the African Savannah, Ungulata has learned to grasp when it runs, it's young, food, objects. Evolution has taught Ungulata a lesson that the chimpanzees in their jungle never needed to learn - when you find something useful, grasp it and keep it, it might be a long time before the next one. The troop carries things with it as it moves, bones, pieces of wood, the rotting rind of a melon, shreds of meat, a stick.

Abruptly, the dominant male of the troop breaks from huddle. It barks loudly to gather the pride's attention, waving its stick. The stick is over eight feet long, crooked, but sharp where it snapped off from a branch. It's tiresome to carry, but the dominant male has never let go since it found it. The lions look up, ears flattening. A female is whapped across the face. The other males in the troop are swinging bones, pieces of wood, broken antelope horns, barking and crowding. There's a tense standoff, the troop versus the pride. Then the lions break away, scowling and growling.

The troop barks angrily, moving forward, surrounding the kill, keeping a wary eye on the lions. Eventually, they settle down to feed. And when it's time to move, they carry the pieces of the carcass with it.

The Savannah is a barren place, the troop eats grass when it must, the offal of its fellow grazers, sometimes at night its members creep stealthily among the herd suckling stolen milk, licking the blood from opened wounds.

***

A hundred thousand years later, Theropithecus Ungulata is still out there on the plains, still loping. But it's spread now.

The species is colonizing oasis and river valleys, finding its way along shorelines, even skirting the edges of marshes.

Ungulata has spread out along the coasts of Africa, all the way down to the south. From Africa, to Asia, to the edges of the Steppe where they gaze in wonder upon the Mammoths and their endless plains.

The deep forests and jungles are denied to them, there are too many other primates, far too well adapted, too well established. These environments are too stable. But in the uncertain climates, the transient biomes at the edge of the Savannah, Ungulata has proven to be a ready opportunist, invading and colonizing. Population densities have gone up, particularly in these blooms of opportunity. Ungulata has become a facile tool user, exploiting its environment in a variety of ways. A barking gibbering language has developed. Troops have become tribes, become villages.

They are the First Men.

***

Another hundred thousand years have passed. Sarkomand, the first city of the First Men has arisen, above a mighty river. There are other cities now, but Sarkomand is still the first and greatest. From across Africa, Asia, Europe, the First Men make their pilgrimages, fasting, worshipping strange new gods, bringing gifts, building wisdom.

The First Men have races dividing them now. Out in the thin places, the lopers have become Leapers. Elsewhere in dry places, the lopers have become Dancers on the plains of Leng, protected from heat and cold by swaddling robes.

The civilization of the First Men is imperfect. Living in their density, in towns and cities, a form of mange has become common. Many prefer the night. Agriculture is an imperfect thing, the First Men never learned to grind grain into flour, they have little patience for cultivation or domestication. Their package has been cobbled together, wild and cultivated, sea and land, offal, detritus, insects and carrion. It's not nearly as effective as later men will develop, the population rises and collapses. But the First Men endure, their civilization builds from one height to another.

The First Men do not cross the sea, however. There are things in the Sea, powers more active then than now. Implacable and alien things that the First Men have found it wise to avoid.

But that is only the beginning. They've learned that there are other things. Malignancies in the deepest jungles, and cold intelligences as slow and relentless as the glaciers they inhabit.

Once, long ago, the First Men lifted their snouts to gaze upon the stars, now what lives between those stars looks back. The First Men have been noticed.

***

Sarkomand is burning. Bloated purple spiders float through the air, made of not-matter, plucking victims from hanging web strands. They've brought things with them, things that cannot be seen, but devour nonetheless.

The First Men left in Sarkomand skulk in their own catacombs, devouring carrion worms and gnawing on their own dead. Their world is being taken from them.

In the deepest, darkest places, the shreds of the First Men, the wisest of them, the maddest of them, the ones with blasted souls and no hope, gather the shreds of knowledge, the stories of strange intelligences, of cold entities. There are bargains that can be made....

***

Sarkomand is rebuilt. But it is no longer quite the city of the First Men. Oh, they still walk its streets, and the pilgrimages still come from across the old world. But there is a tremulousness to the steps, a tendency to pause in their loping gaits to look over their shoulders. To listen to voices

What Devours Also Hungers – Page 84

not of sound, to watch for strange angles, and things not quite matter.

The First Men have climbed to new heights, in art, in literature. By the night of the moon they dance and leap in revels. Sarkomand grows down now as well as up, delving deeper into the earth into catacombs, tunnels, networks. It's as if the First Men are fleeing their own city.

Everywhere, the cities of the First Men wither on the surface, clench and grind and burrow. The First Men no longer want any part of the sky. The open Savanna is now a hateful empty place, abandoned to the hominid apes.

There are new gods among the First Men, although they are not really gods. The First Men no longer worship, but they do bow. They no longer pray, but they do beg. They do bargain and plead. The First Men no longer address the sky, but it's too late, now things in the shadows and voices in corners that shouldn't be, speak back to them anyway.

The First Men know things now.

They know what lies in the oceans and walks among the glaciers; they know where the fabric of the world is rotted, and what dwells beyond. They have looked into the past, conversed with the races that have gone before, peered into the future, seen the Men that will come after them, they are both appalled and amused to see the scummy, wayward, blind apes that are their heirs, and they have seen creatures who come after those.

But it's no longer quite their world any longer, and they aren't quite the First Men any more. The shadows are growing longer and longer. They close off or seal the rotted places, the empty zones of the world; their heirs will not sup from the same poisoned wells.

The Gugs come, brutal and crude. The war is savage. In the end, they are dispatched. But things have been woken, things have been called. Bleating shapeless things are on their way, and no matter how deep the First Men dig, no matter how they struggle or abase themselves, fate lies upon them.

Sarkomand will endure long enough for the new men to walk its empty streets. Sarkomand will be remembered long after the First Men have abandoned their last city.

***

The New Men have come, descended from another lineage of primates. Apes this time, learned to walk upright. Crude and foolish creatures, ungainly and graceless.

The New Men will even build new cities on the forgotten ruins of the cities of the First Men. The remnants of the First Men now haunt those forgotten tunnels, venturing out only to partake of the cemeteries and graveyards for their repasts. The new men boldly have no fear of the sky, but the First Men know what waits out there.

The New Men have no further need for their departed, and the First Men who are left are always hungry. But it's futile.

The First Men know how long and how steep their decline will be, the abysses to which they will descend. They have already seen their future.

But the First Men, some of them, the idealists and dreamers, will remain, hiding in caves, in deep places, in crypts, waiting for the New Men. Trying to teach them, to guide them.

And they know how futile will be the fate of the New Men.

The End

Secrets

Mike was used to getting his pornography in plain brown envelopes. That was why, when the magazine arrived, he opened it up without noticing that it was not addressed to him.

"Secrets" the magazine's title blared redly, on the cover was a nude body in a ditch, so savagely mutilated that for a moment, he could not tell her gender.

Somewhat perplexed, Mike sat down on his dirt-grey couch, in the dim apartment, and began to leaf through the magazine.

He turned the pages with mounting horror and incomprehension until he came to the centre spread. His gorge rose, and he raced for the bathroom, leaving a widening trail of vomit in the hallway.

The centre spread was of a nude, blonde, fourteen year old girl, hanging on a hook, her toes pointing inwards as they dangled in the air, her internal organs spilling past them in glistening ropes, hanging from her eviscerated torso.

Mike returned to the living room slowly. Carefully, without looking at the image, he closed the magazine, and then sat on an easy chair away from the couch, staring at the publication.

He was acutely conscious of his heart pounding, of almost needing to gasp for breath. His apartment had never seemed so small and dark, so wetly claustrophobic.

Who would send him something like this? He wondered. It seemed in abominably bad taste.

For a few moments, he tried to convince himself that it was just some grotesque movie magazine. He'd seen them on the stands, when he was surreptitiously looking at pornographic titles. Magazines like "Gorefilms" and "Horrorzone", they had seemed to specialize in repulsive horror films, publishing the latest visual products of latex, air bladders and fake blood.

Somehow, he could not believe it. The centre spread looked too real. More than that, it was too visceral. Something truly awful had made that picture.

Stretching out to turn the face of the magazine towards himself, he read the cover, "Secrets" it said. "the magazine for the dedicated hunter" read the subtitle.

Cautiously, he flipped it open, carefully reading the index. The articles listed at first made no sense to him. "Black Widow Tips," "Conversations with a Century Man: After the First Hundred."

Others began to introduce a horrible insight. "The Bundy Retrospective," "Transforming for Torture, Renovating Your Bathroom Chamber," "The Taking of Shona, a feature with pictures," "My First Time, Disposing of the Body," that last was designated a humour feature.

And there were the photo features, mimicking conventional pornography with devilish glee, as they touted a succession of mutilated bodies.

There was no publisher's masthead. In fact, there was nothing on the cover or inside pages to give any clue as to where or when the magazine had been published, or who had worked on it.

He was looking at a magazine for serial killers.

Mike felt his stomach lurch again at the thought. Serial killers, mass murderers of all sorts, were part of the fabric of everyday life, he thought. But they were malignancies.

Festering boils on the public body. Isolated events cropping up from time to time.

They can't talk to each other, Mike thought. He found the idea infinitely repellant.

They can't be organised, Mike thought. It felt like an abyss was opening up just behind him. A sane world had suddenly twisted to show a new and horrific face.

They can't have a magazine, Mike thought. A magazine suggested that rather than being a series of individual aberrations, serial killers formed a community. In his mind individual atrocities seemed to somehow coalesce, to merge into a nightmarish whole greater than the sum of its parts.

Abruptly Mike got up and swiftly walked to his apartment door. He checked to make sure it was locked, and then swiftly put the chain on. He studied it for a second, and then, in imitation of old movies, tried to wedge the back of a chair under the doorknob.

He went to the sliding doors in front of his balcony. His apartment was on the twelfth floor. He carefully parted his curtain slightly to view the small balcony. Bare windswept concrete, his ten speed bicycle, an unused mini-barbecue. Nothing. He locked the glass doors.

Then he went from room to room, turning on every light in the apartment. He turned on the television set. A raucous living room opened onto his, and a sitcom family began to squabble. He turned up the volume, finding comfort in the normality of the ignorant program, and then turned on the radio as well.

Finally, bolstered by the normality shining and blaring through the apartment, he returned to the magazine.

It can't be real, he thought. But there it was, the cover glossy under the living room light. It seemed somehow smaller and less menacing in the brightly lit apartment.

He checked the wrapper. As he half expected, there was no identifying mark on the plain brown envelope.

This did not surprise him, because he was too timid to regularly buy magazines off the rack, he had several subscriptions to pornographic magazines: "Gash," "Pink," "Hot Bitches." None of their wrappers gave any evidence of the contents.

The envelope was addressed to Mark Hapman, who lived on the ninth floor.

He put it down. What was he supposed to do? He wondered.

Should he call the police on this Hapman fellow? But surely it wasn't a crime just to receive a magazine? Was it?

He thought uneasily of his own collection. It was not, he thought, a large collection, or anything like that. He did not consider himself obsessed. He only collected a few titles, although he had sent away for various "Special Editions: Not Available on Newsstands!!!"

What was and was not legal? He wasn't sure. What if the police inquiries extended to him, and his locked filing cabinet?

He catalogued and stored his magazines in a filing cabinet he kept in his bedroom. Although nobody ever came to his apartment, he kept the cabinet locked at all times, just in case someone were to visit.

Wasn't it illegal to open someone else's mail? He wondered. Perhaps far from this Hapman fellow being in trouble, he would be the one facing charges. And anyway, Hapman would not be happy if he called the police, not happy at all.

Was this really a Serial Killer magazine? Maybe it was just a species of unusually sick or gruesome pornography, he rationalised. Just because the pictures were there, didn't mean that people had been murdered for them, they were just special effects. Even if they were real, it didn't mean that the murderers had taken the pictures, they could be police photos.

Without coming to any firm conclusions, he put the magazine away in the empty bottom drawer of his filing cabinet and watched television relentlessly until four in the morning. Twice he had to switch channels when the station he was watching ceased broadcasting. He watched television with an almost physical intensity, avoiding any further thought of what lay at the base of his filing cabinet.

Mike was exhausted and bleary at work the next day, barely able to keep up with the hectic workload. The day's activities left him little time to ponder the magazine.

For most of the next week, he was able to push the magazine from his mind. Mike worked with single-minded intensity, and at home he busied himself with one hobby or another, or watched television with almost studied concentration.

He approached his work and his hobbies with the focussed absorption of one who didn't really know how to talk to people. He could relate to people as they flitted around the margins of his tasks and goals, but found himself uncomfortably silent when conversation drifted away from the matters at hand.

He liked to think he was good at small talk. But in fact, his range of subjects was limited. People were often discomfited by the way he would attempt to force conversations in certain directions, voicing opinions they had heard before.

He was vaguely aware of his social limitations. This impelled him to focus even more strongly on work and hobbies. Outside of their structure, he was uncomfortable. At the occasional staff party or social function, he shyly stayed in the background, quietly drinking himself to intoxication.

So, he was quite able, by sheer will, to avoid thinking about the magazine and its disturbing contents.

He did, however, determine that Mark Hapman was no longer in the building. Hapman had moved out two months ago and, as far as he could determine from the caretaker, had left no forwarding address.

But it remained there, in the bottom of his cabinet. Towards the end of the week the arrival of another unmarked brown envelope, this one his usual fare, forced him to think about it.

Time had taken its jagged edge off. It couldn't be that bad, he reflected. It was just an atrocity magazine, he decided, as he flipped through the pages. Now that he had steeled himself, its photographs lacked their earlier stomach turning qualities, though he still shuddered with repugnance over some of the more extreme shots. Pictures which, from their crude execution, gave the images a disturbingly realistic cast.

Its fascination with visceral horrors, whether real or staged, was not actually an endorsement. No more he thought, than the panting slut's depicted in "Hot Bitches" actually degraded women as a whole.

I mean, he thought, it's just a magazine. They are all just magazines. Even a magazine for serial killers...no, he corrected himself...about serial killers is just a magazine. He replaced it in the base of his cabinet.

There couldn't possibly be a magazine for serial killers.

The next day, at work he broached the subject.

He made it a point not to dawdle when lunch hour came, instead he went directly to the cafeteria, hanging around until Roger and Neil filled their trays and then joining them.

Mike had few if any friends, though he considered his co-workers friends of a sort. He never stopped to wonder if they felt the same way about him. In truth, he had little idea of what to do with friends.

Roger and Neil were co-workers who tolerated his presence with careful politeness. They did not actually dislike him, rather they found him excessively focussed on work, and usually with little to say that was not connected to it.

"I saw a program on TV," he said, "about serial killers."

They looked at each other. This at least was a new topic.

"They're really popular, in a gruesome kind of way," Mike continued, "the program said there was even a magazine about them... or for them."

He waited to see if they would take the bait.

"I don't remember seeing that in the listings last night," Neil said doubtfully.

"Channel 17," Mike lied, "at eleven thirty. But isn't it weird though, I mean: A magazine. What do you guys think?"

"I don't think it's that weird," said Roger thoughtfully, "if you get enough people with a specific interest, a magazine would form. Hell, a whole culture forms."

"Look at your own hobby, Mike," Roger waved his fork, "Ham Radio Operators. You have a bunch of people with a common interest. An esoteric technical knowledge. It's nice to talk shop. You form associations, have magazines, conventions, develop your own language, get to know each other, go on social gatherings. Voila: A subculture."

"There's all kinds. Professional associations, science fiction fan clubs, counterculture groups. They are everywhere you look, hundreds of them."

"Our culture is drowning in subcultures," Neil volunteered, "the main culture is breaking up into some lowest common denominator dishwater. Cultural values are being replaced by subculture ethics, or their lack, look at gangs as an example."

"But could you have an illegal subculture," Mike persisted.

Roger shrugged, "like Neil says, look at gangs. There's a lot of interest in the dark side of human nature. They used to make heroes out of wild west outlaws and depression era gangsters."

Janine passed their table, carefully looking away. Mike coloured. He'd had a crush on Janine at one point. He'd sent cards and flowers, phoned her continually. One day, two large male relatives of Janine had arrived at work and explained to him that his attentions were not wanted. They had not made threats, but he had felt threatened all the same. He stopped. He felt hurt and embarrassed by the episode. It made him feel stupid, and vaguely angry.

"That's only about them," Neil pointed out, "there are actual illegal subcultures. Gangs and motorcycle clubs for one thing. The mafia. The drug subculture. Prostitutes have a common language and identity. You know what disturbs me most?"

"What?" Mike asked.

"Child molesters. I can't imagine people that could be further underground. But they find each other. They become pen-pals. They trade pictures and pornography. They even share victims. Every now and then you hear about it, pornography that moves halfway across the continent, rings that are exposed from time to time. It's like there's a network. It makes me sick."

"It sort of makes you wonder why they do it," Mike stuttered, "take such risks, I mean. You'd think they'd keep to themselves."

"Affirmation," Roger said, "I guess it's easier to justify when you know you aren't the only person doing it. Sharing it makes it all right, somehow. I guess they need a society."

"Yeah, but," Mike persisted, "do you think there could really be a magazine for serial killers.

They both looked at him blankly for a minute.

"Doubt it," Roger said. From there on the conversation turned to their subjects and he was unable to force it back.

The first article he'd read had been a 'handyman' feature. About converting the bathroom into a torture chamber. Later, as he sat on the toilet, he'd looked at his tub. The chrome fittings were too easily broken, he realized. He could see how easy it would be to replace them with brass, to fit brass handles into the walls. Countersink screws would be required to bear human weights. He could see, suddenly, from the article, how simply and beautifully it could be done. Sound absorbent ceiling tiles. Simple electrical extensions.

A medieval torture chamber in plain sight. It could be converted and no one would be the wiser, even when they were using it. There was a surreptitious attraction to the thought.

Roger and Neil hadn't helped, he decided, as he leafed through the magazine again. He was looking at it more and more these days. The photographs had lost their power to disgust him, though, he admitted, it exerted a kind of bizarre fascination.

The centre spread, for instance: The victim hadn't simply been killed. The fascination of the image lay in how it had been done, the absolute mastery of the murderer over the victim was chilling and at the same time riveting.

He still wasn't sure what to make of the magazine. Or what to do with it.

What was it really? He wondered. For serial killers, or simply about them.

The articles convinced him.

He read the "Disposing the Body." It was all about the befuddled attempts of a murderer to get rid of his first victim without attracting attention. The body had been at home, the killer hampered by nosy neighbours and the lack of a car. His solution had been a series of increasingly powerful blenders, and the liquefied remains poured down the toilet.

Mike had been shocked to find himself laughing out loud at points, as he read the article.

The classifieds at the back held their own perverse fascination. Snuff tapes, photographic portfolios, both licit and illicit, were offered, sometimes at astounding prices.

Here, for instance, was the "Canadian Series" for a thousand dollars a video.

Elsewhere, "Classic 16 millimetre snuff" was advertised.

"Authentic Holocaust Prints." It sounded almost legitimate.

"The Orlock diaries." What in hell was that?

Invariably, he would put away the magazine. Locking it securely. Promising himself that the next time he took it out, he would dispose of it one way or another. It would be time to resolve the issue.

His attempts to locate Hapman, tentative as they were, had failed completely. He considered mailing it to police headquarters, and washing his hands of it, but was afraid they might somehow trace it back to him.

Somehow, he could not bring himself to destroy it. Partly, he felt, it was because he needed its existence as proof. Proof of what? ...that it existed. That things had been done. It would be like destroying evidence.

Sometimes he thought it would be a shame to destroy it, it was so professionally done, typeset on glossy paper, it was technically the equal of anything else in his filing cabinet. Perhaps more than equal.

Mike's indecision about the magazine occupied more and more of his thoughts. At work, to his co-workers, he seemed to become even more withdrawn and aloof. His careful avoidance of Janine, eroded by his distraction, faltered, and only his repeated embarrassing and humiliating brushes with her caused him to pay attention to his environment.

The magazine continued to exert an increasing spell over him. He no longer paid attention to the rest of his carefully hoarded pornography. Unmarked brown envelopes arrived, and were left unopened and unheeded.

Mike now felt that he could consider the magazine with almost clinical dispassion. He leafed through the "Taking of Shona" the pictures and text depicting the abduction, rape, and eventual murder of a female hitchhiker. It was structurally and stylistically simple pornography, distinguished only by its subject matter. It held no power over him, he felt, save the unyielding puzzle of what to do with it.

It did not disturb him that he had an erection.

Two weeks later, the policeman arrived.

Mike was vaguely surprised, and mildly insulted to find a motorcycle cop filling his doorway. He had rather expected them to come in a squad car.

"Mike Connor?" the officer asked. He was huge, over six feet tall. He seemed somehow inhuman, the hard glistening surfaces of the leather boots, white helmet and mirrored sunglasses, together with the huge blocky frame giving the impression of some titanic beetle masquerading in human costume.

"Yeah," Mike said, swallowing hard. Just looking up at the man made his chest feel tight.

Without asking the Officer stepped inside, emotionlessly surveying the dim apartment.

"We have information leading us to believe you received a magazine a few weeks ago," the Officer made the statement a form of question, pregnant with dark answers.

"Um," Mike wasn't sure what to say, or do, "I think you should look in the kitchen. The fridge."

The Officer briefly surveyed him, from mirrored glasses, and then stalked into the kitchen.

Mike followed him. At least, he thought to himself, it's over. The most disturbing part of it all was that, in the end, it was not disturbing at all. It was perfectly normal. Completely reasonable. It was. It simply was, that's all.

The Officer opened the refrigerator door.

Light spilled out. On the first level, beside the milk cartons and the ketchup, sitting in a bed of lettuce and tomatoes, garnished with sliced mushrooms, was a severed human head. Blond hair with dark roots swept along the edges of the lettuce. Whitened eyes screamed silently. The mouth was stuffed with a peach.

He'd wanted to use an apple, but it wouldn't fit. In the end he'd settled on a peach, and now, it seemed appropriate.

The face and hair were covered with congealing strands of viscous whitish fluid.

The Officer stood there frozen, the refrigerator door flung open, staring at the severed head. Mike could feel each heartbeat in his chest, a slow thud that seemed to shake his body.

The biggest surprise had been how easy the actual killing had been. Oh, it had been exciting and difficult, full of fear and adrenaline. But inside him, it had been easy.

It had been there all the time, Mike thought. It's there inside everyone, he thought.

The Officer straightened, breaking the spell. With practiced ease, he swept two cans of beer out of the fridge, sweeping the door shut, and tossing one can to Mike.

There was a liquid fizz as the Officer popped his cans top, and quaffed a swallow, fixing Mike with his eyeless gaze all the while.

"I guess I should put you down for a subscription," he said.

The End

The Vampire's Provenance

The Senator briskly trotted up the steps of Xenos, his steps springing with anticipation. Behind him, his limousine sped off into the snowy evening, to return discretely in a few hours. The doors opened and he was welcomed by the chamberlains. He shrugged out of his overcoat and winter boots and proceeded to the anteroom.

He was surprised to see two other men there. The lawyer he knew and greeted. The lawyer had been and off and on acquaintance for years. He had started out poor and worked his way to a respectable position in his profession. Not the top, that would have been unseemly and ambitious, but close enough to it. The lawyer was a family man, and was always careful to make time for his family.

The Senator struggled with the same problem himself and respected the lawyer for his dedication to his family. His son had died of cancer and now all he had left was his daughter. She was unutterably precious to him.

The other man was a publisher. He was a heavyset man, who looked gaunt, the way cancer patients sometimes did, as if they were hollowing out inside their fat. The Senator had seen him around at social occasions from time to time, but they had never really met. The lawyer formally introduced them. The Senator was amused to note that none of them volunteered their names.

The Patrician entered.

"Gentlemen," he greeted each of them in turn, "I am terribly sorry to keep you waiting. It is a most remarkable find that we have discovered and I wanted to ensure that our surroundings were just right.

He ushered them gracefully into the conference room. They settled into antique leather bound chairs meticulously separated from each other at the burnished oak table. On the table in front of each chair lay an anonymous ledger, bound in fine brown leather, perhaps calfskin. The Senator noted the taste and elegance which permeated the room.

Servants so discrete as to be invisible served tea, while the Patrician prepared his notes. Finally, he cleared his throat softly, and looked up.

"Gentlemen," he announced, "we have found a vampire."

At those words the Senators mouth went dry, he glanced at the others. The Lawyer looked interested, but noncommittal, his fingers twitched, as if wanting to make a few notes. The Publisher was impassive, a great stone face.

"We have gone through great time and expense to research the creature's history," the Patrician tapped his volume, "which we have documented for your enlightenment."

He opened his binder, as if on a signal, the Senator and the others opened theirs too.

"It dates back to 1886, making it substantially in excess of a hundred years old."

The Senator felt a thrill run through him at the thought of such a magnificently old specimen. He looked at the contents of the binder. At the top was a reproduction of an old photograph, what were they called? Daguerreotypes, he answered himself. It depicted a bearded, shabby man holding a rifle that even at the time of the photograph must have been ancient. Standing with him was a grizzled woman the Senator assumed was his wife, and five children, two girls entering their teens, two younger boys, and a small child of indeterminate sex.

"As you can see," the Patricians voice supplied a calm narration, "it originated in the Ozark region among those degraded American stocks we now call hillbillies. These were relics of the initial waves of expansion into the interior following the French and Indian wars a century earlier. They washed into the mountain areas and degenerated to an insular subsistence lifestyle little better than the Indians they supplanted. I daresay, you could find parts of the area today where little has changed since this image was taken."

The Publisher cleared his throat. The Patrician accepted this message and moved on.

"The picture that you see depicts the vampire and her family prior to her conversion. We believe it was taken in 1885, in a small town called Mill Junction, which was a local distribution centre. They were visiting relatives, the family actually lived much farther in the interior, near a hamlet called Putney Creek."

The Patrician looked up to see that he had their attention.

"The old man is the father, Nat Bergheim. The mother is identified variously as Jessie, Jezebel, or Jessica Bergheim, but her own family was the Winstons."

"The boys were Tommy and Lester, the youngest was Mason."

The Senator thought that Tommy looked much like his own son.

"The older sister" a shyly grinning gap toothed girl of perhaps fifteen "was Ruth Anne."

"The younger." the Patrician pressed his fingertip against the face, "became the Vampire. She would have been about thirteen years old in this picture, although with the state of records, it is difficult to say for certain."

The Patrician looked up inquiringly, "Did you wish to hear its name."

Quiet negatives answered. The Senator sipped his tea, watching the Patrician closely. The Patrician continued.

"On the next page, you will find an enlargement and enhancement of the image depicting our nameless child." it showed a serious, dark eyed girl barefoot in a plain burlap dress, partially obscured by her brothers.

"The winter of 1887 was an unusually bad one, that and an epidemic of whooping cough and a local economic depression had brought travel to a standstill."

"You must understand that as a consequence of a traditional and largely illiterate society, the oral history is very good. We had a pair of researchers conduct extensive interviews among the two dozen or so eldest people in the area and found a high degree of correlation both with each other, and with recorded history back well over a hundred and fifty years."

The Patrician coughed delicately.

"Within the approximate time period identified, 1885 to 1890, we find the 'red man`, so called because he was said to have glowing red eyes. He spoke a strange tongue, which we have tentatively identified as Spanish, and was thought to be either the devil or in league with the devil. There were various stories, mostly apocryphal and unverifiable. But we do have one bit of documented information."

The Senator turned pages; most were neatly typed transcriptions of portions of interviews, dealing with the Red Man, or recollections of the Bergheim family. They were rendered phonetically in rural dialect and signed with X's or painstakingly printed names. Christian Wessle, Mamie Dickers, Joshua Gum and others had told their tales and scrawled their names. He came to a page that was obviously a photographic reproduction of faded script on ancient parchment.

"One John Summer Walters, a sheriff's deputy, had occasion to report a lynching in the village of Preachers Hat. This is midway to Mill Junction from Putney Creek, but I would hasten to add not a direct route."

"A villager, Peter Haddo, encountered a dark man molesting his wife. A fight broke out, and the man, Haddo, getting the worst of it called out for the rescue of his friends, who came running and soon overpowered the Brute who was strong as a bear and equally fierce. They took him for the Red Man who has caused so much trouble in these parts and such misery to Nat Bergheim, and believing him guilty of deviltry commenced to hang him, but he bounced and struggled on the rope so long they took him down and burned him. He took an uncommon time to die properly. Afterwards no one would speak out, and as it is probably a Negro, no charges will be laid. July 7, 1887."

The Patrician turned the page. "Note the reference to Nat Bergheim. This is the one of the few direct connections we have between the Red Man and the Bergheim family. We believe that this was the Progenitor Vampire, probably a Spaniard though its antecedents are uncertain."

The Senator allowed his eyes to drift to some lines of transcript.

"I: Maizzie, did you ever hear of any tales of the Red Man and the Bergheim family?"

"M: Nuthin' bout the Red Man bear hearin' of, an less bear speakin'. There's lots of stories."

"I: What about the Bergheims? Were there tales about them, any of them?"

"M: Don you speak bout Nat Bergheim. He was a good man, a Christian. He wouldn' let the Red Man through his door. Bad luck happen to him, that all."

"I: What happened to him?"

"I: Maizzie, what happened to Nat Bergheim and his family?"

"M: Git out of ma house."

The Senator returned his attention to the Patrician.

"In the spring of 1887, probably the early part of May, the unnamed girl sickened and died. The onset of illness was gradual but quickly accelerated. Local opinion seems to have attributed it to consumption or tuberculosis. She was buried without incident. But within a month the other children began to take sick."

"Mason, the youngest died first in June. Followed by Lester at the start of July. Both Tommy and Ruth Anne were showing symptoms by this time. Those symptoms were rather vague, a general wasting away, fatigue, exhaustion, listlessness. On July 10, 1887, Nat Bergheim gathered his family and took them on a two day trip to Mill Junction to see a real Doctor."

He tapped the Binders pages.

"Here are the rather uninformative notes of that visit. The Doctor prescribed fresh air and saltpetre. The Bergheims returned home, Ruth Anne was left behind with relatives who had a marriageable son."

"Ruth Anne improved quickly. Tommy did not. He died a week after the Bergheims return to their homestead. Both Nat and Jessie appear to have gone a little mad after that. Perhaps the first sign was his determination that Tommy should not have a normal burial, but instead, should be covered by the heaviest rocks that a man could lift. The community was shocked, but assented to his wishes."

"Nat took to carrying a gun around with him at all times, even in the home and building a fire just outside his doorway. He refused to go hunting, but instead, traded his meagre belongings for fresh meat. Other hunters in the area reported the woods were haunted and it was unsafe after dark. Especially around the Bergheims. We have reports of Nat Bergheim firing his gun in the night at nothing."

"Jessie's condition was quieter, but no less disturbing. At times she would scream and weep and tear her hair out. But more often she would sit in her chair, and rock back and forth, holding conversations with her dead children, as if they were gathered all around her."

"Jessie deteriorated much more quickly and showed many of the symptoms of her children. By mid-August, through the Ozark telegraph, Nat Bergheim called his daughter Ruth Anne back to care for her mother. She brought with her a strapping young man by the name of Zeb Crane. From local descriptions, quite a catch. He was tall, good looking, well-muscled, a likeable boy and excellent hunter."

"Unfortunately, the families run of bad luck extended to young Crane. No more than a week or two after arriving he disappeared while hunting. Two weeks searching by the villagers of Putney Creek turned up no sign of him. Years later a couple of boys discovered what was thought to be his rifle while playing near the Bergheim place on a dare."

"Ruth Anne suffered a relapse. With two sick women to care for, Nat Bergheim appears to have lost whatever fragile hold on reason that he had. There are stories of him staggering around drunk and raving in the middle of the village, screaming like a madman. His friends and neighbours ceased to visit any more, though they left baskets of food at his doorstep during the day. Nor did he leave the house, instead barring and bolting the doors and windows. Towards the end, he allowed no person within fifty feet of him when he ventured outdoors."

"The end came quickly. By the beginning of September, Jessie had died, the family had been reduced to one frail girl and her father. The shock of the death seemed to jolt Nat Bergheim back to sanity, and he spoke calmly and rationally. If his insistence that she be buried under a mound of stones as well seemed odd, it was not half so awful as his misfortune, and the villagers were glad to assist him."

"A few weeks later a friend came to visit. He had heard several shots a few nights before and had resolved to make inquiries. What he found, they say, turned his hair white and addled his mind for the rest of his life."

"Nat Bergheim had gone mad once again, and shot his daughter in her bed. He had, in fact, reloaded and shot her twice more; although once would have been more than sufficient. Her right arm was separated from her body and lay on the floor. He had then fired several more shots inside the house, blowing holes in the door and windows. Finally, as the dawn rose, he settled into his rocking chair, drank a bit leaving the jug at his right side, smoked one last pipe of tobacco, leaving it in his left hand, he put the barrels of his shotgun in his mouth, and pulled the trigger. The villagers found him that way, rocking gently back and forth in the breeze, without a head."

The Patron paused and took a sip of water before going on.

"So much for the folk stories of what occurred. The cabin has since fallen down and returned to nature. In fact, all the towns mentioned thus far exist only in local memory. I would assume however, that Nat Bergheim wishes regarding burial were respected in his own case, as a visitor to the site identified as that of the house found six stony graves. The largest was excavated and disclosed a headless skeleton. Partial corroboration, Gentlemen. Nothing else but the graves would indicate that anything had ever lived there."

"Six graves." the Lawyer commented.

"That is correct, Sir, in a family of seven." the Patrician replied, "one would assume the Vampire was buried more conventionally. Certainly the stories fit into the classic patterns of Vampire predation, with the undead returning to feed first upon its own family. These rustics had no tradition dealing with the undead, and certainly would not have understood what was happening to them. Knowledge of Vampires and Vampirism would not have reached into the area until at least the late 1930s with cinematic monsters."

"I would venture to guess that on Nat Bergheim's final fatal night, it was not his daughter Ruth Anne that he shot at, but something else, something that fed upon her."

"Perhaps he recognised it, and that was what broke his mind, for surely, in his unlettered, unformed way, he had suspicions. The stone graves confirm that."

"He shot at it and killed his only living daughter and then it turned its face to him, blood dripping from its grinning lips, and he saw what he could not possibly understand or accept."

The Patrician paused, gauging their reactions.

"But forgive my melodrama. It is all speculation. There is only one that might know what happened that night, and she is not the sort that volunteers information."

"Putney Creek began to experience problems. Livestock went missing. So too did several children. A few of the young people seemed to catch the wasting disease. As the winter wore on, more and more people began to abandon their dwellings and congregate together in a few large houses near the church. By all accounts it had been a poor summer for crops and hunting. The winter that came was harsh and savage. Overcrowding combined with malnutrition and privation contributed to deaths. The Church bells tolled through the winter."

"The next summer was no better. By the time a fourth summer had rolled around Putney Creek was abandoned. It is an interesting curiosity that the residents had taken to burying their dead under mounds of stones. Some of them were so large they must have been dragged by oxen and taken two men to lift. The tradition is a singular one, it began with Nat

Bergheim and ended with Putney Creek. Nowhere else in the region do we find such unusual burial.”

He allowed himself a pause.

“Well, one exception, the stories hold that the Red Man was buried beneath a mound of stones. But we were unable to verify a grave site.”

“We know it’s a vampire.” Said the Publisher. The Senator winced at the display of poor breeding. “Finish the pedigree.”

The Patrician allowed himself to briefly wrinkle his nose in disdain.

“Well, obviously a successful vampire leaves few footprints. To leave stories behind, evidence, to be recognised for what you are would inevitably lead to extinction. Had Dracula been a real vampire and Van Helsing had not killed him, the publication of a novel would surely have done him in.”

“This creature has not survived a century by being obvious. To perceive its tracks one has to look at the record, to find its red thread in the history of illness and violence and rural mystery that it passed through.”

“I must say that this creature was somewhat different from its kind in that it moved about. Usually a vampire will stay very close to the place of its death, seldom venturing more than a dozen miles away. Even if its food supply abandons the area, the vampire will remain, degenerating into a howling spectre preying on rats and leeches for its nourishment, until it finally perishes.”

“This one moved. It moved into Putney Creek. It almost certainly moved into Mill Junction where the Doctor reports a number of cases of the wasting illness that had scourged the Bergheims. A number of widows and widowers living alone died or disappeared. The rest of the elderly took to abandoning their old homes and joining their families. A priest appears to have recognised the problem in 1893, even if he did not quite understand it."

The Patrician turned a page.

"Here are his journal entries in Latin and their translations. Quite illuminating if you read between the lines.

The Senator allowed the Patrician a small smile at his little joke.

"He personally consecrated and prayed over every house that the wasting illness appeared in."

"Further down the Valley, on October 18, 1894, we have a newspaper account of a small farmhouse being found abandoned. The people and livestock were gone, there was a crop ready for harvesting, clothing, tools, even kitchen utensils had been left behind. They had all been healthy and hale a month before."

"The next article is from a neighbouring newspaper. November 25, 1894, a young man, Willard Hickory was returning home and apparently attacked by a beast or beasts. He was described as torn open 'in a most awful way', with blood everywhere, but otherwise, and I quote 'not much eaten.' How understated."

"Blood," the Lawyer spoke. In contrast to the Publisher his voice was well modulated and questioning, "I would not associate blood with a vampire attack. Rather, its absence."

The Senator turned back to the Patrician.

He shrugged. "It is a popular misconception that a vampire drains its victim in one attack. I am happy to say that such voracious creatures would put such pressure on their food supply that they would soon be discovered and eliminated. More typical of vampires is that they only take a quart or so to last them for days or more. Most victims could easily survive one such loss. It is the third or fourth feeding which usually proves fatal."

"If a vampire was cunning enough to find a family and to move from one member of a family to another each feeding to give its victims time to recover, why they might last a month or more before dying."

The Lawyer raised an eyebrow, to signify that his question remained.

"It was, once again a harsh winter, few people travelled, and fewer if any travelled at night. The reports and rumours that could potentially be assigned to vampiric activities dwindled. Ergo, we assume that the creature had begun to starve. Ergo, when it finally located prey it attacked like a wild animal. But even gorging itself it could not have consumed more than three or four quarts, which left a healthy amount to splash around in the snow."

"I would again call your attention to the phrase, the body was 'not much eaten.' Quite unlike what one might expect from the attack of a wild animal. The attack was attributed to a wolf or bear and a number of hunts were organised to slay the creature. Unfortunately, no bear had been seen in the area in five years, and no wolf in forty, their hunts as reported in subsequent editions," here the Patron turned pages "turned up nothing."

"One man disappeared on one of the hunts, even though he was a seasoned woodsman. His body was found later that summer quite close to his home."

"She survived that winter, though. Farther down the valley there is a folk song called 'Red Eyed Girl.' Its original date is unknown, but seems to derive from the turn of the century. You will find a transcription of its lyrics and notes." the Patrician struggled here, seeming pedantic.

"It deals with a young man torn between his childhood sweetheart and a mysterious stranger known as the "red eyed girl". One passage is particularly revealing:"

"Don't need no red eyed girl,

don't need no sweet night kisses
Just want my blue eye baby come by day."

"This was found in a published collection of folk music from 1915 although the song is older. The publisher's notation suggests that it was advice to girls to go to bed early and be virtuous, rather than to stay up all night, kissing and getting red eyes from alcohol and exhaustion." The Patrician smirked.

The Senator allowed himself a sigh. The Patrician straightened up.

"Outside this area the song became increasingly popular and was gradually transformed to "Red Haired Girl" the form it is known in today in most places."

"It was around this period, 1898 to 1905 that she left the valley altogether and began to feed in the industrial towns of the eastern seaboard. We believe her feeding habits changed to reflect the greater availability of food. She no longer fed on one victim or family of victims to the death, allowing us to search for mysterious disappearances of fatalities, although those still occur, if you should look to the pages."

The Senator shuffled the pages, now a series of newspaper excerpts, and journal articles.

"Here is an interesting story from the Inlands Register from May 11, 1909, it seems workers were attracted by shouting in a secluded alley behind a boarding house. When they came to investigate they found a large portly man struggling with a small girl. Let me read this:"

"Even though quite overmatched she seemed to give a good account of herself and the man was bleeding profusely from face and hands as a result of her having bitten him. The workmen soon set upon the man and rescued her from their attacker, whom they proceeded to set upon for a good while until stopped by the arrival of police. The man has been charged, after claiming that the girl tempted and then attacked him. Police are searching for the girl."

"They never located the girl, although police records indicate that they searched diligently for two weeks."

The Senator flicked through police notations.

"In hindsight," the Patrician reflected, "I would say he was probably quite a lucky man."

"Tracking her becomes more difficult generally, the clues more indirect. We have a mysterious disappearance of an elderly couple in 1910 in Gardham. The death of a hermit in the adjacent town of Whiteridge in 1911, and the disappearance of a spinster together with all her cats, some twenty in number, a few months later. In 1913 there is a sudden spate of deaths at an orphanage in Greenbluff."

"But mostly, Gentlemen, we look for diseases now. Now we see the great Cholera epidemic in Gardham in 1910. In 1915 we have a typhoid epidemic in Portsbridge, the authorities publish a circular seeking a suspected carrier. She is described as, and I quote, "a slender girl of thirteen to fourteen, dark haired and shy, with a doll which she carries." Remember that doll gentlemen."

The Senator noticed that the Patricians voice had slowly been picking up its pace, its accent growing more clipped. The Senator recognised and approved the speaking device even as he was carried along on it.

"In 1917 we have the great 'fatal measles plague' in Evanston. Eleven young boys die, fifty-two are brought to deaths very door in spite of the most stringent quarantines and the best medical care, by what should be an innocuous childhood illness. No known vector or carrier is identified, and the lesser mystery, besides why the children are dying, is how it spreads from child to child."

"In 1918 we had the great influenza epidemic. More than twenty million people died nationwide. If you take out a map of the eastern seaboard and plot the deaths you will find a small dark core where the flu is particularly fatal, and you will find that core moving steadily from one town to the next."

"You see, Gentlemen, in only taking a quart or so she does not kill her victims. But she weakens them significantly, making them much more susceptible to accident or disease. And she carries disease from one victim to another."

"AIDS." the Lawyer stated.

The notion shocked the Senator and he could feel his palms sweat.

"No," the Patron responded, "we've tested for it and found no traces. We believe that she transmits disease from one victim to another, but does not carry it herself. She is like a dirty needle," he smiled, "it doesn't get AIDS only passes it along, once cleaned its harmless."

The Senator turned a page, the litany of newspaper stories and medical reports was interrupted by a breathtaking charcoal drawing of a girl sitting on a set of steps.

"This is the work of Jerome Coldwell, a Bethlehem artist and bohemian who lived between 1902 and 1942. He enjoyed wandering into the slum areas of Bethlehem and making charcoal sketches. After his death his family donated his works to the local museum. This one dates from July 8, 1924. Look closely at the girl."

The Senator turned back the pages to the photographs at the beginning of the ledger. The two faces were identical. A calm unsmiling face, dark sober eyes, tousled hair.

"Notice the doll."

In both the drawing and the photograph the girl was holding a doll by its arm in her left hand.

"Almost forty years and five hundred miles later, and we have her here, unchanged," whispered the Patrician.

"After this, we must go back to our indirect methods. There are no more pictures, or sketches, no folk tales or garbled eye witness accounts. Just a steady incidence of plagues and disappearances, as she wanders the back roads of America, anticipating the methods of serial killers by forty years and more."

"How many?" the Publisher asked. The Senator and Lawyer winced visibly.

"Pardon?"

"I don't care." said the Publisher closing his book, his eyes looked unpleasantly hungry, gleamed with obscene lust. "You've got her tracked from her first period to last Tuesday. That's fine, I don't need all the details. Just the bottom line. How many victims has she killed?"

In spite of himself, the Senator found himself licking his lips.

The Patrician closed his eyes, he held his palms flat hovering over the ledger.

"There is no way to know for certain. It depends on where you draw the line. How many did she kill in a first attack? That died from repeated feedings? That were so weakened by blood loss that they succumbed to accidents, drowning, staggering in front of cars, driving accidents, machine accidents, infections, getting lost and freezing to death? How many were weakened by feeding and then died from diseases that she passed on? How many others died from those diseases?"

He paused.

"Thousands." he said simply.

"Thousands." said the Publisher, something like a sigh escaping from him.

The Senator shivered in disgust.

"I want to see it." the Publisher said.

"Yes, I think it's time." said the Lawyer, "I think we are all satisfied with its Pedigree."

The Patrician spared an inquiring glance for the Senator who nodded slightly.

"Very well, there is more, but perhaps that can come after the viewing. Please, bring your binders."

As the Senator closed his, he noted that the inside of the back cover sported a tattoo. It was only a small imperfection however, and in its way, quite appealing, thought the Senator.

Together they got up and proceeded from the conference room down an exquisitely draped hallway illuminated by indirect lamps. They came to doorway that the Senator recognised as steel with wood inlay. The Patrician had his hand on the door.

"I can assure you all, that it is quite safe."

None of them had the slightest doubt of that, this after all was Xenos.

"Enter then." and they filed through.

It was naked, that was the first thing the Senator noticed. It had pert adolescent breasts with little pink nubbins for nipples. Its skin was smooth and pale, unmarked by blemishes, and its splayed legs did not hide its thin wisps of pubic hair and pink labia.

It was spread eagled on its back, tied down with ropes winding elaborately around its arms and legs. It wore a muzzle that prevented its jaw from moving, its teeth were distended.

The bed itself was a canopied affair of red satin, and its head rested on silk pillows, the room itself, although the senator hardly noticed, was a subdued arrangement of dreamlike fantasy focussing on the bed. An elegant whore's chamber.

"...the ropes are soaked with garlic resin and laced with silver thread, to prevent her from breaking out or shifting shape, but otherwise not unduly harming her. The bed structure itself is reinforced steel and she is securely anchored." the Patrician was saying.

"Can it speak?" the Lawyer asked, he stood at the side of the bed, beside the Patrician.

"It can, it tried to tempt one of our staff into letting it go. But otherwise it hasn't said a word. It indicates no recognition of speech or words. We don't think it really understands in the way that you or I do, or that it is truly conscious. It is merely cunning, and language is just one of its tools for obtaining prey. It's just an animal."

The Senator stood on the other side of the bed and looked at it. Its body reminded him of his daughters. But its eyes were different, flat and glassy, with less animation than you would find in a fish. Dead eyes. They looked no less dead when they shifted to stare at him, just flat and empty. Windows of the soul, looking out from an empty room.

"...disembowelled one of our men capturing it, but we have it completely neutralised. We don't believe however, that we'll break it, or that it will ever be completely tamed. Still, there is a certain excitement in that..."

The Senator noticed a doll in the corner of the room. It was an old Raggedy Ann, so old that all the colours and features had faded. It seemed out of place in the otherwise expensively finished room.

Just an animal, the Senator thought. He could feel himself sweating as it watched him. The dark eyes from the daguerreotype and the sketch stared at him, but without life.

Did its nostrils flare at the scent of him? Its lips work slightly around its muzzle? He felt his pulse racing. A hundred empty animal years, of moving and hunting, a hundred years of flat dead eyes. It's just an animal, he thought. It writhed slightly in its bonds.

The publisher stood at the foot of the bed, looking up its length with hungry eyes.

"Its hymen is intact." said the Patrician.

"Is that an effect of its condition?" the Lawyer asked.

"No, when they come back, they come back with circumcisions and stretch marks, and whatever else they brought with them to the grave." the Patrician explained, "Even after death, a number of forms of scarring tend to be permanent, such as missing fingers, that sort of thing. I believe that this sort of injury would fall into that category. It's all in the physical and medical report at the end of the pedigree."

The Publisher took a deep breath, he seemed to need one.

"You see now why this is such an extra-ordinary find. Even for Gentlemen of such...unorthodox tastes...as yourself, this is an opportunity that comes by once in a lifetime. You understand why I showed this to you as a group, rather than individuals." the Patrician said.

"Yes." the Lawyer whispered, as if he did not trust himself to speak normally.

"This specimen will afford any and all of you much use," the Patrician went on, "but there is a prize here which will only be available once. Who will bid first?"

"Me!" said the Senator, his mouth dry, his palms moist and stomach tight, he had a fierce hot pressure in his loins as he rasped hoarsely, "Me first."

The End

Time in a Bottle

Hardesty waited in the reception room of the Arizona Fusion Research Institute and read magazines.

He didn't particularly want to be there. The Arizona Fusion Research Institute was the retarded stepchild of high energy physics.

For twenty years they'd stubbornly plodded down one obvious blind alley after another, producing a thin trickle of scientific papers and methodology reports which were astounding in their sheer ineptitude. In Geneva, AFRI publications were routinely used as examples of sloppy procedure and poor conceptualization.

Which, Hardesty thought sourly, was why they were offering him an obscene amount of money to visit.

"Doctor Hardesty," a mellow, almost effeminate voice, piped, "I'm sorry to keep you waiting. My name is Seldon Glazer; I'm the head of administration here."

Hardesty looked up.

"We're just thrilled to have one of the world's foremost experts on measurement analysis here to assist us," Glazer gushed.

Hardesty stood up to greet the short balding man. Well into his forties, the little man was swaddled in baby fat; he seemed like the sort to sweat perpetually. His eyes shone with the gleam that Hardesty, in his travels through the American south, recognized as that of a hard core religious fanatic.

"Doctor Glazer," Hardesty offered, taking a sweating palm in his.

The little man blushed.

"Oh," he said, "it's just Mister Glazer. I'm not one of the scientists here. Although..."

Here it comes, Hardesty thought.

"I kind of fancy myself an amateur theologist. So, I'm sort of a scientist."

Not unless, Hardesty thought, you can measure it, dissect it, or subject it to statistical analysis. Otherwise you're a bozo looking at clouds.

Hardesty released the hand, still smiling genially, as he wiped it on his pant leg.

"So," he said, "do you have any real scientists around?"

"A few," Glazer replied, not quite picking up the irony. "Perhaps you'd like to see our facilities."

Hardesty nodded, and Glazer led them off on the tour. As they walked down corridors, occasionally peeking through doorways. Glazer kept up a steady stream of chatter. His almost manic babbling struck Hardesty as somehow false, as if, underneath it, lay a profound insecurity or fear.

"We're all quite thrilled to have you here, you know. We're very impressed with your record."

"Uhm," Hardesty replied, looking around. They were in office spaces, he noted. From the few open doors, they didn't look too bad, good windows, carpeting, lots of shelves.

"Very eclectic background," Glazer was saying, "a brilliant career in small particle work, before you went into astrophysics. You're a real renaissance man."

Hardesty winced at the term. "Actually, I always thought of it as a fairly linear progression. I was looking for insight into the fundamental nature of matter, which lead me to the big bang, which leads to the search for its residues."

"Oh," said Glazer, not really understanding, "so how does this relate to your work with measurements?"

Hardesty winced again.

"Well, strictly speaking, we can only really understand the universe through observations. Human faculties are limited, so we have to build instruments to observe and measure effects."

"Of course," Glazer agreed vaguely.

"So the measuring instruments themselves are inherently limited. Crude, internally biased, with margins for error. The tools we use are flawed and give us a distorted picture of the universe. Everything we do is looking through smudged glass. Only by carefully monitoring or cross checking our results, our measurements, can we work towards an even halfway decent picture of what's really going on."

"Ah," said Glazer, coming up short. "Here's one of our real scientists. Doctor Sam Saddler."

Through an open doorway, Glazer waved at a lantern jawed pipe smoking figure, who waved back and motioned them in. The office was a typical scientist's domain, buried in paperwork. On the walls were full colour star charts, and dominating them all, was a giant, computer enhanced image of the face on Mars.

Hardesty glanced at the poster, and deducted a few IQ points from his estimate of Saddler.

They walked in. Saddler shut down his computer and leaned back in his chair.

"Hello Glaze," he said. "Who's your friend?"

"Doctor Hardesty," Glazer introduced, "I'd like to present Doctor Saddler."

The two men exchanged handshakes.

"So, what are you up to, Sam?" asked Glazer.

Saddler shook his head.

"The usual." He turned to Hardesty to explain further, "it's a private project of mine. I'm looking for signs of intelligent life in the universe."

Don't look in Arizona, Hardesty thought.

"Essentially, I'm theorizing that the universe is inherently unstable, and that consciousness acts as a sort of regulator. It enhances stability.

"So, I'm trying to map out areas of space to measure relative levels of fundamental instability. Those areas, like our own, with the highest levels of inherent cohesion are most likely to support intelligent life."

"What do you think?"

"May I be honest?" Hardesty replied.

"Sure," Saddler said.

"I think you're out of your mind. I think it sounds like one of those nutty cross disciplinary exercises that creation scientists like to engage in. You know, trained in geology, pronouncing on biology, otherwise expert men dabbling in fields they aren't competent in."

Glazer froze, like a deer caught in the headlights.

Saddler just burst out laughing.

"My Doctorate is in Astrophysics," Saddler said, "and I cut my teeth on deep space."

Hardesty shrugged.

"And you're making unprovable assertions that the laws of physics are dependent on perception on a massive scale," Hardesty replied. "That's as thorough a butchering of Heisenberg as I've ever heard.

"Besides, the notion fails logically," Hardesty continued. "If consciousness is needed to maintain the conditions for its existence, then how did those conditions come about in the first place, and how did they last long enough?"

"You tell me," Saddler offered, smiling.

Again, Hardesty detected a trace of uneasiness. Saddler was smoother; more polished, but underneath there was a subtle edginess much like Glazer's.

"It all comes back to religious posturing."

"Really Doctor," Saddler said, "you don't believe in a supreme consciousness setting everything in motion? You look at a watch, but you won't believe in a watchmaker?"

"It's not necessary. Consciousness isn't the cause of the universe, it's just a consequence."

"Is it? Haven't you ever wondered how perfectly right everything is? How this one planet always had the perfect temperature and the perfect atmosphere to maintain life?"

Hardesty shrugged, "you're invoking the Gaea hypothesis. That's a far cry from your universal consciousness."

"What about how versatile carbon is, or even water?" Saddler persisted. "If their properties were just a little bit different... If water contracted rather than expanded when it froze, like everything else, ice would be heavier than water. It wouldn't float. It would sink to the bottom and the oceans would be thin films of brine over immense glaciers. Life couldn't exist at all.

"When the universe began, why did it turn out like this? Why did the physical laws settle into this form? Why did three dimensions grow and six more withered? What created time? The very fabric of the universe is based on a succession of unlikely coincidences, all the forces in balance. It can't be an accident."

"And if the strong nuclear force had been just a little stronger nuclear reactions would take place too quickly for stars to form," Hardesty fired back, "and if it was just a little weaker then protons and neutrons wouldn't bind and stars would collapse, but not ignite. So here we are, stuck between a cold dark universe and a hot short one.

"Anyone can play that game," Hardesty said.

"Easy," Glazer said softly, it was almost a warning.

"Oh yeah," Hardesty laughed, "and why haven't you won the lottery? Why did the guy down the street win? A coin has to come up heads or tails. Someone has to win the lottery.

Someone has to get struck by lightning. Some sort of result had to happen. This is just the way things turned out."

Saddler sat back and grinned.

"Seen the last few readouts from Hubble?"

"Who hasn't?"

"There were quite a few stars missing," Saddler said.

"What?" Glazer asked suddenly, a gleam of terror shining through his genial mask.

"All that shows is equipment error. Faulty imaging, flaws in computer coding, bounces off the ionosphere."

"You think so?"

"Go back and properly re-evaluate the old records; they'll just confirm what we're discovering now."

"That there are twenty per cent fewer stars in the galaxy than we calculated?"

"Bad calculations."

"Maybe they're just going out?"

"And what? Their light disappears at the same time, in flight? Or maybe they're synchronizing for our location, so that they only appear to vanish together?"

Saddler laughed, "Maybe."

He stared at Hardesty.

"You haven't been working with stellar physics much?" He made it sound like a challenge.

"Not for a few years. My real work has been in analysing fundamental constants," Hardesty replied easily.

"Excuse me?" Glazer asked.

Saddler glanced at him, like a steely eyed gunfighter favouring a kid.

"Fundamental constants," Saddler explained, "are the basic unchanging values that physics is based on, the speed of light, the energy value of a proton, the strength of nuclear forces and their ratio to each other. Basic quantities that allow us to analyse and predict the physical world, in the same kind of way that we can add two and two to get four."

"Except that it turns out they aren't so unchanging," Hardesty said.

Saddler turned back to him. "There's talk you might win the Nobel Prize," he said softly.

Hardesty smiled.

"There's talk," he replied.

"This is what Doctor Hardesty did," Saddler explained, "he took a good hard look at stuff everyone had taken for granted, and he found it wasn't fixed numbers. There was a bit of variation there. As it turns out, it's just possible, according to Doctor Hardesty, for two plus two to equal five."

"That's an inelegant way of putting it," Hardesty said. "But not fundamentally incorrect."

"So tell me Doctor," Saddler focussed on him, "why weren't other people noticing this? Like Newton, like Einstein. Why are you only coming up with it now?"

"For a long time, instruments simply weren't precise enough. We just picked up a value and assumed it was fixed."

"Instruments got better," Saddler said.

"Yes, but the fixed values were biased into them. You'd have to cross reference carefully to find the variations."

"Hard to believe," Saddler said, "I've read your papers; some of those variations are pretty big."

"My work is controversial," Hardesty admitted.

"It undermines a big chunk of modern physics. Wallace over at University of Calgary published a paper arguing that if your conclusions are correct, the big bang couldn't have happened."

"I've read Wallace," Hardesty replied.

"I've got an interesting notion," Saddler said, "if you'd care to hear it."

Hardesty shrugged.

"The constants were fixed, but they've started to vary in the last few years."

Hardesty laughed out loud. "But that would mean that the universe is beginning to unravel at the seams. How? Why?"

"I suppose we should take him down," Saddler said.

Glazer nodded.

"Take me down?" Hardesty bristled. He had pegged them for religious flakes. The ungodly sum that had brought him here was starting to seem insufficient.

"Not like that," Glazer said. "Downstairs."

"Where to?" Hardesty asked.

"You have to see it for yourself," Glazer said.

They lead him out of the office and down the corridors.

"Let me guess:" Hardesty laughed, "What is it you've got? The aliens from the Roswell crash? Or maybe it's the genuine shroud of Turin? A stardrive? A working time machine? A wormhole gate?"

Saddler smiled and gave a humble shrug.

Soon they were passing through the experimentation wings. Hardesty noted rooms full of antique computer banks, technicians working busily. Incomprehensible machines.

"It happened in nineteen sixty-three," Glazer said suddenly, "It was an accident really, it probably couldn't be reproduced. There was an experiment with a radically new kind of containment field, there was a power surge and..." he shrugged.

"It was an Eisenfeld magnetic bottle," Saddler said.

"Oh come on," Hardesty scoffed, "I've seen the tests, those things collapsed instantaneously."

"Only," Hardesty continued, "the Arizona Fusion Institute kept plodding down that blind alley. Christ, have you ever looked at your own test results?"

"No blasphemy," Glazer warned. There was an edge in his voice.

"We wrote them," Saddler said. "Our budget is functionally unlimited; almost everything anyone hears of us is a blind, an elaborate bit of misdirection."

For a second, Hardesty was taken aback. What was he saying? That they were frauds?

"I've seen the records, listened to the tapes. But I can hardly imagine what it was like back then, as they struggled to hold the field together," Glazer whispered.

"At first, they just thought they had some runaway reaction, they were afraid of losing the state, maybe a piece of the continental shelf." Glazer laughed at the triviality of it all.

"They're all dead now," Saddler said. "The selfish bastards. Now we're the ones holding the bag."

They passed through barricaded doors.

"I mean, nobody quite realized what it all meant, until a few years later, when test results started to go wrong."

"It was as if," Saddler continued, "the Universe had started to unravel, as if some inherent stabilizing force had been withdrawn."

"Or inadvertently captured," Glazer finished for him.

"Excuse me?" Hardesty began to protest.

"You ever pass by a construction site, Doctor," Glazer asked, his breath rushing out of him. "They have these little windows you can poke your face into to see. Suppose someone was there on the other side, and as you poked your face in, someone grabbed you by the nose, and they had such a good grip on your nose, you couldn't get free. They'd just have a little piece of you, but in such a way that you couldn't bring your strength to bear. Effectively, you'd be paralysed."

"That's sort of what happened here," Saddler said, "we isolated some sort of motive element."

"Excuse me," Hardesty said, aghast, "do you realize what you're saying."

"The instruments are accurate," Glazer replied, "they always have been. The fundamental constants used to be fixed, they aren't any longer. The Universe really is unravelling."

"But that's insane, and if the Universe really is disintegrating because of something you did, then why doesn't it start here first?"

"We think consciousness stabilizes reality as we know it. We think consciousness exists as a sort of reflection."

"In his image and all that?" Hardesty scoffed.

"Probably more like an unintentional by product, like a shadow cast," Glazer replied softly.

Hardesty took another look at the little man. This was an amateur theologist? Hardesty wondered at the bleakness of the viewpoint.

They arrived at the doorway. It was a huge steel bank vault. Strangely, there were no guards. Saddler and Glazer began to turn the locking wheel.

Delusional, Hardesty thought, the whole place was delusional. If they really had what they thought they had, why weren't they celebrating? Why were they hanging onto it?

The door swung open. Hardesty could see a glow inside.

He stepped through the doorway.

"This place takes up some thirteen per cent of the power output of the entire United States," Saddler's voice whispered behind him.

He didn't hear. All his attention was focussed on the unbearable brightness contained in the magnetic bottle.

He felt an overpowering attention focus on him for an instant, then pass on, like a wave. He felt the sensation of a colossal awareness, a being that dwarfed him in its immensity as a mote was dwarfed by a mountain.

And in it, spilling out, he sensed rage. Awful, titanic, terrifying rage. Something immeasurable, incomprehensible, implacable. An unforgiving anger so enormous of breadth and vast of depth that he knew he was feeling but its barest shadow. He found himself weeping in terror, his heart pounding with fear and shame. He found it hard to breath.

Compared to this...nothing compared to this. Lucifer and the whole revolt, he thought, had been a spat; the flood, a minor housecleaning; the transgression in Eden, a mere annoyance; Sodom and Gomorrah was a passing itch that had been scratched.

The anger of the thing in the bottle was beyond human conception, its wrath directed against the whole of the specks who had somehow trapped it there. There would be no forgiveness from that rage, no escape from that measureless infinite wrath, nothing and no one would be spared.

Abruptly, he felt himself yanked back, the door slammed shut in front of him. The terrible roaring was cut off. Not ended though, he could still feel it sweeping through him, like the faint echo of the ocean in a seashell. He knew that now that he had experienced it directly, he would hear it for the rest of his life.

He noticed, abruptly, that he was weeping. Crying in huge sobbing gasps. Tears running wildly down his face.

He looked at the two men, for the first time, profoundly aware of their hellish torture. He shared it now.

"We've made," he said, "a terrible mistake."

Grimly they nodded. Years ago, men proud or lucky had captured something, and the universe, without its steadying hand, its guiding eye, had begun to disintegrate.

"We can't go back," Saddler said. Hardesty nodded, no they couldn't just undo things. Not after he'd faced the terrible rage of the thing in the bottle, not after he'd sensed its hideous, infinite, omnipotent wrath. Anything was preferable to letting it free, to releasing the unfathomable vindictiveness of a limitless, all powerful being.

Even the death of the universe.

But it would get out eventually. The stars would go out and the speed of light would lag, matter would go strange, particles would liquefy and waves would shimmer. Eventually, the very physical laws that allowed them to hold it would weaken and lapse. And then it would be out. Out among the obscene little specks that had dared to cage it. He shivered with raw undiluted fear.

Hardesty wondered how long it would take? How long they had left?

The End

New Age Rising

The face in the clouds stared at him. Its mouth opened and a tongue of smoke descended, searching for him. At the tip of the tongue was an eye

* * *

In New York there is a pyramid of corpses three hundred feet high. Helicopter based telecasts buzzed around like flies while studio computers flashed estimates of the number of bodies in the pyramid based on volume. Surface of the pyramid squirmed as rotting flesh inside the pyramid liquefied and shifted.

Telephoto lenses showed a surface of contorted limbs, emaciated torsos and sightless faces frozen in mute screams.

New bodies were continually being added. Some of the bodies that joined the pyramid weren't quite dead.

Something was being born in there; a news announcer was saying, voice crumbling into static.

No one knew what.

Schroeder's eyes snapped open and the jungle closed in.

* * *

Naked, the fat woman danced in the centre of the village. There was a small man on her back. He seemed to be melting.

Sweat rolled down the small of Schroeder's back, pooling there. Sweat collected at the end of his nose. It was night, and supposedly cooler in the jungle, but heavy moist heat offered no relief. His heart raced keeping time with the desperate erratic rhythms of the drums.

"Do you see it, Schroeder?" Elysse whispered beside him. "Do you see it?"

He could barely hear her whisper above the chants of the villagers. He felt almost ill; the air seemed to writhe around the dancer, like the heat shimmer on a dry road.

"It's the heat," he said aloud. Not caring if Elysse understood. Schroeder felt physically sick, nausea crawled up the back of his throat. He swallowed desperately.

The woman lifted her leg up high, and then brought it down, reminding Schroeder of sumo wrestlers, except faster, jazzier. Her whole body vibrated. The man on her back struggled and squirmed. He seemed to be screaming. She ignored him, and kept on dancing.

He was definitely sinking into her body, his legs, his lower torso gone, his arms melded with her flesh. He was just a sweat shining back and a screaming head.

The ground was rippling around the dancers. He could see it now. Concentric circles of distortion. Ripples. The man caught his eye for a moment, as he sank out of sight, disappearing into her without a trace. The naked woman paused in her dance, gasping for breath, pendulous breasts and heavy brown body glistening with sweat.

The drums, the chants stopped. In the silence his body was unbearably loud, a cacophony of heartbeats and tremblings and breathing blaring from a wrapping of floppy sweating meat.

"Oh God," he moaned.

"Not God," Elysse said, "magic."

There was a hunger in her voice.

* * *

In Havana, Cuba, a cat spoke at great length and with profound eloquence on the nature and value of life. A maddened crowd burned it anyway.

People everywhere shunned contact with each other, especially with strangers. They wore gloves to keep their fingers from melting together.

What Devours Also Hungers – Page 132

Dreams swept the earth, active voracious creatures, they leaped from victim to victim, sometimes not even waiting for sleep. Executives in office towers looked out their window and watched nightmares pursue muggers and victims alike. They licked their lips and planned on trapping wet dreams.

Schroeder staggered across Memorial Plaza, a featureless expanse of concrete. He was conscious that he had no shoes. A wind blew up behind him, he turned...

* * *

Schroeder opened his eyes. It was cooler now, and quiet. Even his own heartbeat was barely visible.

Elysse was sitting beside him, she changed the cool cloth on his forehead.

"Are you all right?" she asked.

"I need a cigarette," he said suddenly, and then realized that he hadn't smoked in five years.

She shook her head.

"Do you remember what happened?"

Schroeder squinted. What did he remember?

Ripples.

A wave of nausea slid through him. He convulsed.

Her hand was gentle, holding him down.

"Do you remember," she asked again.

"There was a ceremony..." he mumbled. What was it for? "Solstice or equinox...I got sick, I think I passed out."

"What happened in the ceremony?"

"I got sick, I passed out, I think I hallucinated..."

"What did you hallucinate?"

"The woman..."

"Yes?"

"She was dancing..."

"Go on."

"There was a man on her back..."

"She absorbed him." Elysse whispered.

What Devours Also Hungers – Page 133

"Hallucination," Schroeder moaned.

"No," her face was intense, staring at him, "that was real, I checked the videotape."

"Ripples."

"Magic."

And he was gone again.

* * *

A man helped him to his feet. He looked oriental. The man jabbered incomprehensibly.

Schroeder waited until meaning seeped in. Sometimes it did, sometimes it didn't, it didn't matter any more if people spoke the same language.

There was a roaring in the sky, wind pulled and plucked at their hair and clothes.

"Fields of corpses," the man yelled over the wind, "standing there, like wheat in the sun. A spirit crosses the sky, dead faces turn like flowers, following the sun."

"Please," Schroeder begged, "what do you want from me?"

"Half the world is dead, turned to dust in the wind, or jelly beneath our feet. New things, never imagined, inherit the world...we never imagined...we weren't ready."

They both crouched motionless as the clouds above them formed into a titanic face that seemed to stare intently at the ground. The mouth opened and a tongue protruded, worming its way to earth. There was an eye at the end of it.

The oriental man turned to Schroeder.

"The face," he whispered.

"Oh God," Schroeder whispered.

"Not God," the man replied, "magic."

"Ripples snapping back and forth in time," the man said. He grabbed Schroeder's jacket, he seemed angry and intense. "Chaos refracting infinite fractals faces furnace seeming refractions."

What Devours Also Hungers – Page 134

"What?" Schroeder asked. The meaning was leaching out again. The voice was turning to gibberish.

"Sentience kills faces oscillating tangent. We fuel fires."

He seemed enraged.

"I don't understand," Schroeder said desperately, "I know those words but they aren't making any sense."

The man pushed something into his hand. A tongue of smoke caught him then and began to drag him into the sky. Schroeder looked up.

"Kyoto is gone," the man screamed, coherently.

It wasn't a human face up there.

He looked at the thing in his hand.

It was a nine millimetre Beretta.

* * *

"I thought at first," Elysse told him, "that it was the fruit. You know, forbidden fruit. Like in the Bible."

"Hallucinogens," Schroeder said suddenly. "They gave us their drink, it had hallucinogens."

"No," she said, "it was real."

"Subjective reality," he whispered desperately, "to an inside observer there is no distinction between reality and hallucination."

"It's on the videotape."

"It's an ingrained hallucination then, a recurrent trauma. The same response to the same stimulus, reinforced memory, acid style flashbacks."

Abruptly, he vomited.

"I still think that's part of it," Elysse said. "It makes sense in a way. How does a fruit or seed bearer get animals to eat the fruit, propagate the seeds. Program a desire to eat, program reality into the fruit. It makes sense from an evolutionary point of view."

"What are you talking about?" Schroeder asked suddenly.

"Feedback loops. Alter the internal realities of the animal. Addictions. Hallucinations. They evolved alongside us, we selected each other for compatibility. Everything does. Everything selects everything."

"You aren't making any sense," Schroeder said, "you're jumping around too fast. Slow down."

"Plants evolved with us," she said patiently, "they evolved to be addictive, mind altering, and animals evolved to be susceptible to them."

"All right," Schroeder said carefully. "Now what."

He had a horrible feeling that if he closed his eyes at that moment he would open them ten thousand feet above the Himalayas. He could feel the chilled thin air of the glaciers.

"I thought it was the plants, but they were just symbionts. Its bacteria or viruses, perhaps just self-perpetuating sequences of chemicals. Subjective infections."

His guts heaved and he clenched his bowels against a loose liquid feeling deep down."

"What?" He looked at her for the first time. She seemed gaunt but her skin was puffy and unnaturally slick. There were pustules on her half naked body. Some of them looked like faces.

She has it too, he thought, she's got whatever it is.

Elysse glowed, he could feel her....elation.

"Viruses selecting sentience. Co-evolving animals with bigger and bigger brains, more complex perceptions, more elaborate subjectivities, because that's all there is, you see. Cause is effect."

"Everything is subjective to the observer," Schroeder said, "but people die in the world out there. That's pretty objective."

"Male objectivity," she said, "the holy phallus separating light and dark. The rape of the goddess, the sowing of order."

* * *

Schroeder staggered out of the dugout. Ragged children ran up to him. He almost fell. Behind him, the dugout drifted back into the river.

The Amazon, he thought desperately. I'm on the Amazon.

Past or future, he wondered suddenly, and laughed at the ridiculousness of the thought.

"Elysse," he bellowed suddenly, shocked by his own voice.

An old man was coming up to him. Dressed in black, supporting himself with a cane.

A Priest.

Schroeder laughed.

"Bless me father," he said suddenly. "For I have gone where none should go."

The priest jabbered in Spanish.

A small girl said in perfect English, "the transmission of viruses of discontinuity remains a coded sequence in some form of coherent order. The viruses attach at X chromosomes. Patriarchy was a function of coherent order opposing discontinuity."

The girl looked startled by the words that had come out of her mouth. The Priest didn't seem to notice. Hallucination?

Sibyl, he thought. Cassandra, Delphic Oracles, mad prophets. Visionaries always fasted and scourged, depressing the immune systems and what did they let in?

"She's been here," he said.

Three years ago, Schroeder thought suddenly. Three years ago he'd gone deep into the Amazon with Elysse on a Doctorate project. He'd remembered Elysse kneeling forward in the front of the canoe, as serious as Napoleon.

"Napoleon Chagnon," he said aloud. The first man into the jungle, who'd lived with the Yanomamo.

They'd gone much farther. They'd lived with a people that even the Yanomamo believed mythical. Over three years they'd seeped into their lives and been granted their secrets. Had been exposed to their....

Elysse had gone too far.

He had to stop her.

He had to stop her before she made it out.

Before she let it out.

"Bless me father," he gasped, "for I must sin."

The priest was shaking his wrist.

He looked down.

There was a nine millimetre Beretta in his hand.

* * *

There were lights in the sky and sounds in the earth. There were shapes in the darkness and presences in the deep.

* * *

"The world of the Goddess," Elysse said. He could see in her eyes that she wasn't speaking to him anymore. The words were flowing out of her like water from an overflowing cup.

"Transformation, transfiguration, life and death, birth and rebirth, the warm menstrual flow of eternity, of sky and soil. Of wet fruit in your mouth, juices spilling down your chin."

"Elysse," he whispered, "what's going on?"

There were ripples, he realized. Small ones, but they were there. Ripples in things. Ripples in existence.

"Magic," she seemed to pay attention to him for a second. "Magic is what's going on. It survived here."

"That's what evolution was all about, selecting for magic, evolving for magic. For blending the subjective and objective. For melding real and unreal."

"Magic went out of the world, confined and eliminated by a phallocentric world. Men bound the goddess, bound themselves with rationality, with the illusion of an objective world."

What Devours Also Hungers – Page 138

"There's only one world," he told her. He reached out to hold her wrist, but his hand slid off. It left a greasy trail in the slick phosphorescence of her skin.

"We have to bring it back. Bring back the Goddess. Let magic loose in the world. End the oppression of male reality."

"Elysse," he said, "listen to me. You can't let it get out. The people here are adapted to it, they have resistance. The world out there hasn't had magic for a long time, we've lost our immunity."

"It's a new age dawning," Elysse said.

"It's extinction," Schroeder whispered. She did not care.

"A glorious one. The end of patriarchy. The end of order and hierarchy and structure, of male logic and male domination."

Schroeder closed his eyes and saw carnage, cities choked with corpses, storms and horrors, a world racked by cancer, crippled and howling by a plague it could not begin to understand.

He felt himself detaching. Becoming unrooted in time and space again. Felt the awful gravity of events pulling at him.

Flickering consciousnesses bursting in and out of existences, propagating each other at unimaginable velocities. Unprotected human souls fueling a supernatural firestorm, a psychic holocaust.

Was there anything out there, waiting to feed? Or was it really just us, he wondered, pent up and ready to explode? Growing more and more volatile and intense over millennia to compensate for magic growing weak and faint?

Response becoming more sensitive as stimulus, the viruses, grew weaker. Was it cause or effect, he wondered. And what would happen when pure magic was released back into the world?

No defences, no resistance, no way of coping. Time pulled at him, a mad dog biting itself in convulsions.

With a physical effort he held onto his body, onto his moment in time and space.

"Elysse," he pleaded, "don't."

She smiled beatifically, her body swollen and oozing with an infection of magic, a ripe fruit long forbidden to the world. She was choking on the viruses of a new age.

"I have to bring the gift, don't you see. The gift of magic. I have to set it free."

He was suddenly aware that there was something cold in his hand. For a second he thought it was the wet cloth she'd had on his forehead.

Then, in a moment of crystal epiphany, he knew what he had in his hand.

A nine millimetre Beretta.

The End

The Perfectionist

"REAL LIVE CRIME: The highest rated show on the airwaves. The dark face of the video revolution. Now all you had to do to get your fifteen minutes of fame was to commit your darkest atrocities to video...and send it in. No fakers please, we're looking for the real thing."

Stanford knew he was in trouble when the policewoman met him at the door to the sorting suite. She was black.

Not that he had anything against blacks. Or black women. Or young, black, women police officers, he amended. It was just that he thought those qualities shouldn't go together in a police officer. He just didn't like dealing with the politics.

"Stanford Hope?" she asked.

He nodded and handed her his card.

"Stanford Hope," it announced, "Executive Editor, Real Live Crime Television."

She smiled professionally.

"I'm pleased to meet you. My name is Corporal Phoebe Whytes; I'm the new assignee to the monitor detail."

"I know, Carl told me he was being transferred."

They shook hands, he unlocked the editing suite, marking down the entry codes and comparing with prior entries. Everything seemed to be in order.

He set up the pictures of his family at the workstation. A wife and two grown daughters.

He hoped that this evidence of his humanity would encourage her to be civil. In his experience, most cops weren't.

"So how does this work?" she asked as he settled in. She sat in the chair he indicated.

"It's pretty simple. People send us their zips or files showing crimes being committed. They're transferred to storage chips. I review them, selecting for broadcast, you select those which may assist in investigation."

"There's a lot of chips," she said doubtfully, looking at the mornings stack.

"Sometimes I have to requisition a couple of people to help vet them. This isn't a big pile, comparatively."

"Your TV show basically shows real people getting mugged and raped and killed. Isn't that right?" There was accusation in her tone.

"Sort of the dark side of America's Funniest Home Videos," he agreed with studied neutrality, "we beat them regularly in the ratings."

"Doesn't it ever get to you?" she asked.

Christ, he thought, she hasn't even looked at a chip yet, and she's starting.

"It's a job," he said noncommittally. He grabbed the first chip off the pile, noted the references, and slotted it in.

A leather clad man was using a bullwhip on a screaming woman. He watched for a few seconds, noting that the woman was overweight. Then he made his notes and switched it off.

"Pass," he said dismissively.

"What did you do that for?"

"Home-grown kink, I don't know why they send this shit to us. They should try the S & M network."

But of course, the truth was that this couple simply weren't good looking enough to make the S & M channel.

"I saw blood!"

"Stage blood, not a very realistic mixture either, the texture and hue is wrong."

"I don't know…"

He shrugged.

"If you want to follow it up, I can sign a copy over to you, but the whole thing is so artificial they might as well roll credits at the end."

"Jesus, you're cold blooded."

"After a while you get to tell the real stuff from the fake. There's a lot of people out there role playing twisted fantasies."

"I wonder where they get them from?" she said acidly.

He took a deep breath, but didn't rise to the bait.

"It's always been there. Do you have any idea how many cultures have practiced torture as an art form? The Apaches, the Comanches, the Iroquois, the Chinese, even the Puritans. Ever hear of bear baiting? Or bull fighting?" he said softly.

"I heard the story once, of how the ancient Romans had built a bronze bull with a hollow inside for a slave. They'd haul it out into the Colosseum and then light a fire under it, and as the slave slowly roasted alive, his screams would come out of the bronze channels sounding like the lowing of a bull. Charming eh?" he continued.

"A more common Roman stunt was to dip criminals in pitch, hang them up, and set fire to them. Use them as lamps to light the streets for special occasions. Of course, they probably didn't live more than ten minutes that way."

"But it was the thought that counted I guess," he concluded.

"It's kind of creepy that you know that stuff," she said.

She doesn't give an inch, he thought.

It's going to be a long day.

He slotted more chips. They watched in silence. Most of them were standard muggings or assaults at ATM's or in parking lots. Recorded on building security cameras. There were CCTV's everywhere; it made you wonder why crime was even a thing. But of course most of the time no one was watching. And anyway, the trouble was watching and being able to intervene were two different things.

Once in a while a security guard would arrive on the scene to heroically struggle with the criminal. He tagged those for possible play, regardless of quality of image or subject matter.

The security companies liked it when you showed their employees actually fighting crime. They were more inclined to buy advertising. And of course, it contributed to a sense of public security.

False security, in many cases, actual intervention by security personnel occurred in only one out of 700 recorded incidents.

He noticed her taking notes.

"You don't have to do that," he said, "these files are automatically copied to local law enforcement agencies by the monitoring companies. We have secondary arrangements."

"Arrangements?"

"The network has deals with security monitoring companies like TecSec and ProTech. We pay a licensing fee and a per minute use, and we get our pick of their camera scans. They send us their crime pick ups."

"You get a lot of it?"

"It's about three quarters of our input, but most of it is pretty uninteresting. The odd rape scene in a parking lot, but that's about it. Mostly, it's filler for the main program, and dump for our Freenet."

"Charming."

He sighed.

"It's that kind of world."

Next was a rape scene. Image quality was terrible, low light situation. It looked like the cam had been placed on a dresser, slightly askew, tilting the frame in an irritating way.

The woman was genuinely terrified as the rapist beat and threatened her.

"He's playing for the camera," Officer Whytes whispered.

"A lot of them do," Stanford replied.

Stanford clicked it off and began an automatic copy sequence.

"I've seen this guy before. He's one of our regulars," he told her.

"He's masked."

"Serial rapist. He wants to be on television, but his stuff just doesn't make the grade. You'll find you've got a file on this guy, or at least this M.O. I hope you catch the bastard."

"You get that a lot?" she asked as Stanford popped in another chip.

"What?"

"Criminals showing off."

"A fair chunk of it is that. Not all, some of its security cameras, some of it is just good citizens happening to catch something."

"I don't like it."

"What?"

"You're giving them something to feed off. It's like it inspires them, encourages them."

"That's a bit like blaming the victim, isn't it?"

"I don't see it that way."

"You know, years back there was a television show in which hoodlums set a bum on fire. The next night, some young thugs went out and did it to an old man. They blamed the television show."

"And..."

"The point is that they were just shits. They were going to do something, maybe the show influenced the specific action, but they were still going to go out and raise hell no matter what. Television doesn't make people good or bad."

"It just makes them famous."

"For fifteen minutes," he agreed.

They scrolled through a well dressed black man being assaulted and beaten by a couple of youths in tribal masks who then did a pelvic victory dance around the bleeding body.

The image was obviously from a low end handcam, visibly different from the stationary, wide angled security cams. These were muggers proud enough of their work to try for their fifteen minutes.

They wouldn't get it. Not this time. But he slowed it down enough to examine the camera work and choreography.

Some potential artists here, he reflected.

"You may want this one," he told her, "the victim's identifiably urban middle class. He's probably got a complaint outstanding. This might give you a lead."

She nodded.

"Run me a copy, and I'll send a search through our files."

She paused.

"What about you, are you going to use it?"

"Probably not, black on black crime just doesn't rate."

The minute he said it he could feel her anger going up.

"What!" Her tone made it clear she wasn't asking a question.

"Look, it's not racist," he said hastily, "it's just network iconografix. The best television criminal is a young urban black male. The best television victim is a small white elderly female, or alternately, a white pretty young female. That's what the audience likes."

"The audience doesn't like black on black crime," she snapped sarcastically.

"The audience doesn't care."

"What about white on black?"

"Some novelty value."

"How about Hispanic violence? Or Asian? Is that photogenic?"

"As long as you have a mix, there's some interest. Monochrome violence gets a yawn."

"I can't believe you're saying this. You publicize crimes based on skin colour."

"You're making it sound racist," he said angrily.

"Isn't it?"

"No, it's not. It's simple marketing. Most crime is poor people doing it to other poor people right next to them. Most crime is black on black or Hispanic on Hispanic and so forth.

"That's not interesting to the viewer. The viewer wants the villain to be distinct from the victim. Colour doesn't matter, just the difference, remember Rodney King. If you can't tell the players apart, then you can't be sympathetic."

"Just watch for the one who's bleeding!" she said.

"In commercial terms, the average viewer is middle aged, middle class, white and usually female. They want to identify with the victim, to respond to or enjoy the incident. Ergo, the villain has to be different: Young, poor, male and ethnic." Stanford told her.

"Remember when that sports star, Simpson, got in trouble. The leading news magazine of the day ran him on the colour. They used computer enhancement to darken his skin several shades and add beard stubble. Nothing racist, they just wanted him to look unpleasant and threatening. Like a criminal.

"Its market driven It's not racism, it's just using very broad strokes to paint a picture. Images get reduced to icons.

"I don't care if you use crayons. It's still racist."

They confronted each other for a few minutes. Then he turned back towards the screens and slotted the next chip.

They watched it flick fast forward. It was a domestic assault, apparently recorded by a child in the home. Good copy, television worthy.

She asked for a transfer for police records. She didn't say more than she had to.

There was a poignant image of the mother sobbing and bloody, reaching out for her child afterwards.

With as few words as possible, they worked through the remaining chips.

Homemade porns. Security cameras mutely witnessing tiny atrocities. Bystanders capturing car accidents and burning buildings. Criminals, flaunting their crimes.

A parade of human decay.

"I don't know how you can live with yourself, doing this," she said finally. "Swimming in filth."

Stanford laughed.

"I get that from every one of you," he told her. "You know that? Every single one. You people should grow an imagination."

"You should grow a conscience," she shot back.

"I have a conscience," he said. "I've got a wife too, and a couple of daughters, one's going to med school out of state." He waved at their pictures. "I pay my taxes, do my job, I go to church and I give to the United Way."

"How can you stand to do this?"

"How can you?"

"Because maybe I'll find something on one of these chips that will help somebody," she said.

"Convict somebody you mean," he mocked. "There's a difference. These chips might give you a clue, help you catch a perpetrator, or maybe provide a little bit more evidence to convict one you've already caught."

"So?"

"It's not like you're actually helping any of these victims. The damage is done."

"Then at least these scumbags might not get the next victim."

"Right," he said sarcastically, "we know who gets helped."

"What did you mean by that?" she asked angrily.

"Nothing."

"No. You meant something, say it if you've got the nerve."

He looked at her and then looked away.

"All right, I've seen a lot of cops come through here," he told her. "And most of them have attitude like you do, but what they've all got..."

He paused, she waited, staring defiantly.

"What they've all got is that they're hungry. They're looking for a big break. You know? They all start off outraged, but before you know it, they can't even be bothered by ordinary muggings. They're keeping their eye out for the big case that'll make them."

"I'm not like that," she said, without much conviction.

He nodded.

"I'm sure that you didn't jockey for this detail," he said flatly.

"Well, it's a good career track," she said hesitantly.

Stanford grunted.

"But I want to help people, to make a difference. I know what it's like..."

"Honey," he said, "it's a job. That's all it is. You can do it well, or you can do it badly. But nothing that you do will change what's on those chips, or where they came from, or where they'll end. Let's just get on with it."

The next disk started.

Stanford stared, as the opening scenes unfolded.

"It's him."

"Who?"

"It's the Perfectionist. One of the regulars. We've had other files from him, but before he sends one in, he likes to practice. Carl, your predecessor, told me about it. They'd go back and find that for each file he made, he'd...refined his technique with 'practice victims.' Make sure everything is just right."

The cam swept lovingly over a series of surgical instruments, a nude female figure struggled indistinctly in the background.

"He's been linked to eleven killings. Carl said he seemed to be working on a new routine. He told me about it, how it seemed to be developing. That's how I recognized the opening."

The cam swept over the woman's face as her eyes pleaded and mouth twisted around the gag. Stanford went cold.

The perfectionist picked up a scalpel and went to work.

"Oh my God," he whispered softly.

"What?" she asked.

It was, he decided with a shrinking rational part of his mind, technically perfect. Lighting was good, focus was tight, camera movement dynamic, material and victim...the victim... photogenic. Broadcast quality all the way. It was going to be tonight's headline segment, no doubt about it.

The victim... he thought blankly.

"It's my daughter," he whispered, drowning.

The End

Wyrms

"Hey Sport, take a look," the Prostitute calls, as she cocks her hips and sticks out her tongue.

I'd had some odd propositions, but this invitation catches me completely off guard. I glance at her wet tongue, protruding from her mouth.

There is a sphincter, right in the tip of her tongue. As I watch in astonishment the sphincter opens, exposing a dark tunnel.

"Remarkable." I expostulate, "I've never heard of such a thing!"

She pulls her tongue back into her mouth, concealing it behind a toothy grin. She looks just like a common prostitute, with artificially red curly hair, thigh high boots, and rather too much body covered by too little fabric.

She wears a long coat, which she leaves unbuttoned to expose her charms.

"You like it, huh?" she says, tossing her hair.

"I must confess, it has attracted my attention."

I watch her mouth carefully as she speaks, but I see no further sign of the deformity.

"There's more," she tells me. She steps closer, almost intimately close, moving in that undulating way that prostitutes have. I can smell her cheap perfume.

"Indeed?" I reply

"You wanna see?" she whispers in my ear.

"I might," I say cautiously.

"It'll cost you."

"How much?"

"Just a bill, and I'll show you everything."

Her hot breath holds the promise of things unimaginable. I find the temptation irresistible. I am seized with a curiosity for this bizarre woman that was almost sexual.

"That is quite satisfactory," I agree.

She fits her arm inside mine and leads. We walk four blocks to her room.

Her room is in a dilapidated two story dwelling, of the sort that had been mass produced as a dream home for GI's returning from the war. It has clearly seen better days, and just as clearly not seen recent maintenance. I imagined that the slumlords who owned it had divided and subdivided it into tinier units. It has been a long time since it was a family dwelling.

"My place," she whispers huskily, "what do you think."

As she slides the heavy bolt along the door I look around. There is a lumpy bed covered indifferently with dirty blankets, I notice a cigarette burn in one of the pillows. Beside the bed is an end table, with a derelict clock radio and an ashtray with too many cigarette butts. I observe a couple of suitcases open and sloppily packed, nylons hanging off one side. A door on the opposite side leads to a toilet, and I presume, a shower. It was barren, messy, and smelled vaguely of something I couldn't identify.

Typical whores chambers.

"Quite acceptable," I tell her.

At least, I think to myself, there were no needles lying about.

"The money," she sidles over me.

Pulling out my wallet, and being quite careful not to let her see the contents, I fish out five twenties. She makes the bills disappear. Stepping back, she briskly pulls off her clothes and lies back on the bed. Propped up on one arm, with her legs spread obscenely exposing her sex, she grins at me again.

"What would you like to see?" she asks.

Fully dressed, I sit down on the bed beside her nude form.

"That tongue, to start with," I say.

She obliges.

Her teeth, I discover, merge with her gums, there being no dividing line between hard white and soft pink. She has no apparent collarbones, and the junctions of her arms and shoulders are, quite simply, wrong. Her legs seem to contain too many bones, her feet too few. She appears to lack a proper spine, having in its place, an oddly rigid, articulated band of tissues. Even her navel is an obvious sham.

There is more of course. She opens herself to me, and my probing eyes and fingers find innumerable anomalies. Some subtle, others so glaring as to make one wonder how she passed at all.

"You aren't human," I say, eventually.

She merely laughs in answer.

"You aren't a freak either. Your abnormalities are far too comprehensive for you to be a sport of nature."

She rolls onto her stomach. I cannot not help but notice the perfect roundness of her bare rump, but in view of what she is, I cannot not see it as anything more than an abstraction.

"Which leaves us with science or the occult," I pause, "are you an alien from outer space? Or some visitor from a magical plane?"

She laughs again, it is a friendly sound.

"This is my world as much as yours," she replies, "and further to your next question, I am no supernatural creature."

"Science," I tell her, "has mapped the four corners of the physical world. Where then do you come from?"

"Oshawa," she replies.

My stunned look throws her into a fit of giggles. She quickly stifles them. She slides her hand bonelessly along my thigh.

"Come, be comfortable. Lay down beside me and I'll tell you the whole truth," she laughs again, "no extra charge."

She pats the bed. I sit down next to her, adjusting a pillow in order to recline comfortably.

"We," she said sonorously, "are the children of fabled Mu."

"That paleologan fantasy," I exclaim, sitting up, "an invention of addled theosophists, and I dare say, even they had trouble swallowing their own myths as they invented them."

She turns onto her side, eases me back into a supine position.

"We have no word of our own for it. Our lost land, we know it by chemical memory, not sounds." she explains, "So we must borrow names."

"Maple White Land is far too English, and Atlantis much too human, to describe our ancestral home. Even Lemuria is too..." she pauses significantly, "...vertebrate."

"Invertebrates," I whisper. An alternate line of biology producing a humanlike intelligence. Impossible. But then again, I thought of octopuses with their eyes evolved so like our own, and their almost mammalian intelligence.

"Clever monkey," She stretches out nude on the bed, in a manner too sinuous too describe.

"Molluscs?" I make the word a question.

She makes a face.

"Slime and tentacles? Really, how revolting," she reaches up to run her fingers through my hair, it is an abnormally long reach, "listen, and I will tell you our secrets."

"We were born at the dawn of time, perhaps before even the coelacanths crawled from mud flat to mud flat."

As she speaks, I see it, an empty steaming silent world of primordial green.

"Mu was a continental mass, or subcontinental mass, perhaps the size of Madagascar off dark Africa. It was alone, in those turgid oceans, save for immense Gondwanaland far far away."

"It was Gondwanaland that the lobe finned fishes learned to make a home of the land. But in far off Mu, the vertebrates did no more than visit, instead, the surface was colonised by other forms of life."

The image of the empty prehistoric rain forest is thick in my mind.

"What are you?" I ask.

"The phylum Annelida," she whispers, "came into their own on Mu. There with no competition, they were free to flourish in a vast radiation of species."

Earthworms. Annelids were earthworms.

"The insects, arthropods, were stifled by the limitations of their exoskeletons. But we were not. Herbivores, carnivores, predators and prey." Her eyes took on a dreamy quality. "In the low marshes and in the high trees, we evolved, changing, developing small and large forms, filling every niche, creating new ones."

In my mind the primordial jungle filled suddenly. Worms filled it, crawling in the earth, and on the ground, and up trees. Worms sprouted tentacles, coiled masses of muscle, bifurcations, cilia, a dozen different ways to move about. New shapes appeared, each more indescribable than the last. It was a silent world, for all its surging life, different senses were in use, subtle chemical sensitivities employed, new pathways developed. In the marshes primal horrors hunt and in the trees indescribable things swing. The steaming jungle foliage parts, revealing vast shapes moving across the landscape elephantine in their bulk...

I stand up abruptly. I am sweating profusely. I have the feeling that there's something wrong, but I can't tell what.

She puts a hand on my chest, arm unnaturally long, guides me back until I am lying beside her. My unease passes.

"There is more," she says.

I am curious again.

"What happened?" I ask.

"Millions of years passed."

I can feel the eons like stones around my neck. I long for a glass of water.

"As Mu drifted alone on its tectonic plate, vast Gondwanaland stretched and broke apart. But too late, the vertebrates were established. Mu eventually merged with some wandering continental remnant..."

"And then..." I prompt.

"Mass extinction. Our world's history is full of them, two ecologies meet, one is ground under. It happened most recently in South America, did you know that? A flourishing landscape, South America produced marsupial wolves and sabre toothed tigers, ersatz horses and elephants, and creatures so strange as to have no counterparts anywhere. Then the Isthmus of Panama rises from the sea and for the first time the mirror creatures of mirror continents meet."

She rolls over on the bed and stretches languorously, sinuously, in a way that no human confined by muscle and bones ever could, her flesh twists and ripples with sensuous ease.

"Then all gone, all those fabulous forms, save only for the lone opossum, which advanced into North America."

I move away from her, leaving the bed. I sit down on the rickety chair as she gazes at me.

"It was like that then, too. The giants, the most specialized, the most advanced forms died. One generalized advanced form survived, lived to move among the dinosaurs.

A durable, hardy, opportunistic creature. Mu's equivalent of a rat, if you will."

"That was your race?"

"Our line. Our ancestors. Millions of years passed. New vertebrates evolved, and we evolved as well to prey on them. Intelligence, as you understand it, came relatively late in our history."

"How is it that you appear so human?" I ask. Her nude body sprawls across the bed, but now, as I gaze on it, I see a giant earthworm humped into a parody of female beauty.

She smiles at me. There is something unnerving about that toothy grin, its utter wholesome normality completely out of place in this dank room, with febrous jungles drumming in my head.

She does not answer. Instead she darkens. It is almost imperceptible, like the shadow of a cloud passing over a person on a sunny day. She continues to darken, her features swelling and diminishing, not in the unnerving liquid fashion of computer animations, but in a naturalistic way, if I can use such a description. It was unnerving in the way it was not unnerving.

She stands from the bed, a tall Negress.

"You shift shape."

"A partially open circulatory system, a muscle structure built on bone and cartilage nodules, we held our own in encounters, but the vertebrate form was much more effective in sustained contests. Our life form could not compete in endurance or durability. We evolved new ways to deal with predators and prey."

"Incredible to think that you could exist in human civilisation."

"We are not alone, hiding in your teeming multitudes." Her skin lightens slowly, and she seems gradually shorter.

"South America produced its own parallel humans from new world monkeys, who now exist in secret."

"Surely they aren't shapeshifters," I say.

"No, they have been evolving to resemble humans in the sixty thousand years since your race invaded their continent, and they are adept at hiding."

She pauses.

"And of course there are the fearsome Tcho Tcho people, arisen from marsupial stock. They would not pass a close examination, but none survive who come close enough to them for such an exam. Only remnants remain in Borneo and New Guinea, but some say their ancient city, Leng, in the trackless deserts of Australia is yet inhabited, and unnameable gods are still worshipped in the name of inhuman superstitions."

She is now a young Latin male; I cannot ignore the prodigious erection. She/he follows my gaze and laughs.

"There were even Lemurians, but I think they are now extinct."

The organ detumesces, growing smaller and smaller, her form drifts back to a feminine shape. Changes occur, so many and so subtle that I could not say exactly what they were. I have the physical sensation of my eyes being pulled from their sockets, so unusual was it.

Oddly, however, I am not horrified.

"You must be behind it then. All of humanities legends, werewolves and vampires, demons and fairies, shapeshifters of all kinds."

"This may be so."

Languidly she drifts towards me.

"Are you immortal?" I ask breathlessly, "How do your life spans compare to ours?"

"We have our own spans, and our own version of immortality, in memory, as do you."

She smiles strangely.

"You have spoken of predators and prey. So many of these supernatural creatures are... Are you a predator species of the human race?"

I do not find this thought particularly frightening or abhorrent. Some rational part of me feels that perhaps I should.

She laughs and grins at me, straddling my seat so that I cannot move away. Her form, and her voice, were once again the strumpet who had tempted me.

"Listen," the whore's voice said, "you people watch over each other too carefully to support predators. In any case, there is no need. You do too good a job on each other."

"Us?" she puts her arms around me. "We just like to keep our heads down. Keep out of trouble. We eat at restaurants and shop at grocery stores. We live quite normal lives among you."

"Intelligence," I blurt, "how did your species develop intelligence and language?"

"I think," she said with emphatic seriousness, "that it probably emerged from staying competitive with you and the smarter mammals."

"I think that in the beginning it was simple, everything was chemical, scent based. It was all a matter of making the proper chemicals; we were very good at that. Then other senses came into play. You had to have the right colours, and the right shapes, make the proper movements. As behaviour became more complex, so did we, in order to recognize and mimic it."

"You know, you people are all wrong about language. You used to think that language evolved out of animal cries of hunger and courtship. Then you discovered that those calls come from a different area of the brain than that which controls language."

"I think language evolved from listening to sounds, not making them. I think intelligence is a function of mimicry."

"You imitate us in mind as well as body, then. You are just like us."

I struggle to grasp the implications of what she was.

She takes my hand and thrusts it between her spread legs, forcing my fingers deep inside her. She does not wince.

In spite of myself, in spite of my knowledge, my breath catches in my throat and my pulse quickens. I feel my body respond physically.

She smiles; it is a humanlike expression, of power. Of someone in control.

"We imitate, to pass, but we are not like you. This..." she moves my fingers inside her, "...means nothing for us. To you this invokes primal drives, wired into the core of your being. Sex and reproduction."

I sweat profusely as my fingers writhe inside her wet reaches, deeper and deeper. How deep? Would I disappear inside her? My heart beats like a jackhammer, and I cannot keep my breathing steady. As I look at her nude body, heaving on mine, touching it, smelling it, perceiving its texture, I realize she is now a perfect female, quite indistinguishable from any other female human. She bears none of the abnormalities I had earlier noted.

"We reproduce differently; we are driven by urges primordial, quite different from your own. This," and with a movement of her hips she hunches further down onto my hand, "means nothing to us. Nothing whatsoever. It is no more significant than a tap on your shoulder."

Face impassive, her back arched, her head tosses in a parody of sexual fever.

"If your sex organs are a sham, how do you reproduce?"

"The ones you relate to are a sham. We have our own, we have male and female. The male fertilizes eggs in the female's body..."

Abruptly she pulls away, standing and looking down on me.

"Surely..." I gasp, not quite knowing what to say. I sense she has left something unfinished.

"Look!" she commands.

As I watch, her perfect breasts develop small lumps. They grow and multiply until her breasts were covered by a mass of round nodes. The gentle swells, the nipples are gone; in their place are two pink masses vaguely resembling bunches of grapes.

The ground beneath me seems to swirl vertiginously; each node reveals a slit, which opens to a white orb, with pupil and iris. From her chest, a hundred eyes open to stare at me.

I lurch backwards, toppling my chair, but somehow maintain my footing. Still, my revulsion was not visceral, but has something of an intellectual quality. Too much, I thought, too much to absorb, as I stagger towards the door. Each of those hundred eyes tracks my movement.

She moves to obstruct me.

"Does your kind have psychic powers?" I ask.

"There is no such thing." she tells me. She is between me and the outside world.

"Its chemicals then," I guess, "pheromones. You are controlling my behaviour, my emotions. I should be horrified, terrified, but I'm not."

I make a half-hearted rush for the door. She catches me easily and bears me back to the bed.

"Very clever monkey man." She smiles at me, ripping at my shirt; her hand caresses the bare skin of my stomach. Involuntarily my skin crawls. I struggle feebly.

"We can manipulate primal drives, suppress and magnify them. Fear, lust, curiosity. Monkeys can be so curious, it can override self-preservation." She makes a purring sound in her throat.

"Are you going to eat me?" I ask. Even now, I could not summon panic.

"Of course not," she assures me. Her hands explore me, probing; I am helpless in her grip.

A thought occurs to me.

"The male fertilises eggs in the female's body. What then?" I try to shout, but can not escape the maddening normality of my tones. I feel oddly will-less under her, there is no motivation, no urge, I seem to float.

"This," she tells me in a husky whisper, "won't hurt a bit."

I look down to see her mouth hovering over my soft belly, the tongue lances forth, spearing into my flesh, feeling it's way around my body cavity as it deposits hundreds of larvae.

She lies, she lies.

I find that I have gained considerable weight since then. I have few needs these days, and she sees to them. She is quite comfortable in my presence now, often wearing what I have come to think of as her true form.

I am allowed to feel no horror at the sight. Her world, her true world is a chemical one, the sensing and decoding of complex molecules, an inhuman intelligence of chemistry. And its manipulation.

What is horror but a rush of hormones?

I feel that she enjoys my presence. Daily, she shows me new forms. She whispers in my ear, imparting unspeakable wisdoms that threatens to tear my sanity asunder in spite of her chemical buffers.

Even memory, I have discovered, is chemical, trapped in codes of RNA, transmissible with a touch. My dreams now, are dreams of the primordial jungles of Mu, full of unnameable shapes. I bear the secret knowledge of the worm.

I prefer to be awake. It is not so bad as the ageless memories of her race, and their threat, which swirl in my unguarded unconscious.

Sometimes at night, we lay out under the moonlight, and she caresses my form. Her fingertips tracing the pathways of the things that move ceaselessly now, under my skin.

They will be born soon.

Sometimes, on rare occasions, I am left alone long enough for her hormonal wash to fade away. Then I am finally free to feel the true horror of my situation.

OH GOD OH GOD OH HELP OH GOD OH PLEASE OH

OH

OH

The End

The Squad - Centipedes

LIEUTENANT (Voice Over) - For no other reason than that they did not kill me on sight; I have been given command of a squad of unstoppable killing machines, deathless masked murderers.

My security clearance tripled overnight. You want to know about the President's prostate exam? What they really had down in Area 51? I could get you that. But for these bastards, I barely ranked. The files on the squad had so many black marks through it was like reading confetti.

The parts that I could read, the edited mission profiles, were like the nightmares of a psychotic witch doctor. Speculations about zombies, demon gods, avatars of death, alien. Sometimes wild ravings. I checked the General's medical history. He was on so many anti-psychotic medications his piss glowed in the dark. He would ask for electroshock. He fought to get a lobotomy.

Afterwards, he wrote 'It didn't help.' Mortality rate was 70% among the support crew, two thirds of that was suicide.

Only one thing is clear - whatever these things were, we have no idea. We don't know what they were, or why they were or how they did it. We just know what they do. We are like monkeys with atom bombs. All we know is that we have them, and we can point them at things that might or might not be worse.

I had a mission. The parameters were fucked. Just a code name and a set of GPS coordinates. No objectives, no rules of engagement, no support.

But I know deep down, that none of that was necessary. Their only rule, their only objective was kill. No survivors, that was the one constant from every mission.

***

The Helicopter is insanely loud. Its metallic skeleton, a dragonfly carrying a cargo container. The Lieutenant sits beside the pilot.

LIEUTENANT - Is this the target zone?

PILOT - We've just passed the quarantine perimeter.

LIEUTENANT - Any idea what we are facing? What's the perimeter encountered?

PILOT – No idea. Quarantine perimeter is the zone outside contact. You'd want to talk to field Perimeter.

LIEUTENANT - What do they say?

PILOT - Nothing, they're presumed dead.

LIEUTENANT - Where do we land?

PILOT - We don't land. We just drop the container and they do the rest.

LIEUTENANT - We're not high enough for the container parachute.

PILOT – There's no parachute. They don't like it when we go high.

LIEUTENANT – What?

PILOT - Bombs away.

LIEUTENANT - Wait!

The Pilot pulls a switch, the helicopter jerks as the cargo container lets go, begins tumbling through the air.

LIEUTENANT - Jesus Christ! That's a thousand feet.

What Devours Also Hungers – Page 166

PILOT - Yeah, I feel better already. Hey, are you into woodworking?

LIEUTENANT - Fuck! What? Woodworking?

PILOT - Yeah, I do it to relax. Unwind from those things. I just bought this amazing table saw, 22 inch blade, got it from a sawmill. Knocked half the teeth out, so it does really rough cuts. Just mangles the wood.

LIEUTENANT - What are you talking about?

PILOT – More and more, I've been thinking how restful it would be to just turn it on and lay my forehead against it. You don't think that's screwy, do you?

LIEUTENANT – Jes/

Loud noise, metal grinding, a flash of light, a chemical stench like burning hair.

PILOT - We're hit. We're g----

***

The Pilot's head impaled on a metal rod. That's the first thing the Lieutenant sees when she opens her eyes. Apart from the blood and the steel jutting through torn flesh, he looks very peaceful. The second thing she notices is that most of his body is missing. The third is the acid smell of burning rubber and plastic.

She thrashes, afraid to look down and see whether her own body is intact. Restraints bite into her shoulders. She is still wearing her safety belts, still strapped into the crash seat. She releases the buckles feeling them loosen.

She crawls away, staggers to her feet. Everything is intact. Miraculously, she has survived. Helicopter debris surrounds her.

What Devours Also Hungers – Page 167

In shock, she looks around, seeing a typical, normal Rockwell, middle-American town. The streets are empty, except for a man and woman who appear to be impaled on a double headed parking meter.

She stumbles toward them, staring. They are back to back, leaning against each other. Their faces are contorted in rictus of agony and terror. The man's lower body is distended oddly; she thinks she can see the shape of the edge of the parking meter in his body. Their feet do not touch the ground, they dangle in the wind.

LIEUTENANT – What the fuck?

Her gaze drifts to their feet. Lower. There are pools of blood and guts beneath them, the remnants of their ruptured bodies. The blood still drips down.

Still drips.

Dripping.

This happened recently, the Lieutenant thinks. Perhaps minutes before the crash. Beginning nausea is swept away by a surge of terror. The Lieutenant, heart pounding, draws her sidearm and whirls around, circling twice, searching the landscape.

That's when she sees the thing. At first she'd taken it as part of the helicopter debris. But now that she looks.... this thing was part of no machine. The alien quality of it baffles her at first. Shining chitin, segments, claws. Some kind of .... insect. Was this thing the problem? The Mission?

It's dead now.

Mission accomplished?

A skitter behind her. Ahh, the Lieutenant thinks dispassionately. Mission not accomplished. More of them.

Not insects. Their wobbling segmented bodies move towards her.

The Lieutenant is proud of how calm she is in that moment, how analytical she is, as she mentally catalogues a description. Can they see her she wonders? Or perhaps, like certain predators, they only see movement? In which case, being still would be best. Or maybe they see in other terms, see other spectrums? Maybe they see with sonar, or track with scent?

Whatever it is, the two things seem to register her presence. She watches as they stiffen and orient on her. Hundred yard range? Does their perception work beyond that?

They move decisively towards her. The Lieutenant wonders how fast they are at the same time that she turns to run.

***

The Lieutenant sprints like the wind, it's the fastest she's ever moved in her life, graceful as a gazelle, sure footed as a mountain goat. The ground is a blur beneath her feet. Some part of her feels elevated, flying on an instantaneous runners high, every bit of adrenalin surging through her body. She would feel great, if she wasn't shitting her pants in terror.

In that instant as she turns to run, as she breaks into her sprint, she sees them move in her peripheral vision, knew that on a straight away, they will run her down. So she heads around a corner, leaps a wrecked car, uses that to springboard onto a hanging sign and up on the roof. As she hears them skittering up the side of the building, she's already on to the next building, leaps to a thankfully full dumpster, through an open door, and out the other side.

All it had done was attract more of them. Twistings and turnings, the best run of her life, and every glance from peripheral vision showed another joining the chase. She runs

What Devours Also Hungers – Page 169

along a brick wall, turns a corner, and leaps into a store window, hoping for a back door, a basement, a heavy door that she could slam, a safe she could lock herself into.

Smack into something solid and unyielding. She almost bounces backward, but something catches her shoulder, steadying her.

LIEUTENANT - Holy shit.

It's one of them. One of the Squad. Her mind seizes up in paralysis. Then the training kicks in.

Sawyer, she remembers from the briefing. This is Sawyer. The heavy set one, sometimes childlike, sometimes aggressively sexual, traces of a potbelly, uniform rotting, his mask is made of human skin, and his weapon is a chain saw.

Sawyer stares at her, fascinated. He cocks his head, as if not quite recognizing her.

LIEUTENANT - It's me. Remember the teddy bear? I gave you the teddy bear.

Sawyer cocks his head again the other way.

She feels warmth trickling down her legs. Behind her, she hears the skittering, the things are out there. Sawyer looks up. Then he looks at her. He shakes his head as if to clear it, as if the mystery of her can wait until later.

Almost gently, he moves her out of the way, stepping past her. The things waver uncertainly. She does not turn, merely listens to Sawyer's footsteps as he steps over the store window, glass crunching under his boots. She hears the rev of a chain saw.

She does not look. She doesn't want to see.

There's a lot of noise, she thinks that some of it is the sound of things screaming in high pitched chitin voices.

Then the chain saw shuts off. Patient footsteps walking away.

The Lieutenant is staring. In the mirror of what she now recognizes as a jewelry store, the walls smeared with blood, she sees herself, dressed in fight suit. The shattered remain of her crash helmet clings to her head. Her face is obscured by a mirrored visor.

***

CONTROL - *Please describe the phenomena.*

LIEUTENANT - *I saw two people, I think it was a married couple, impaled on a parking meter.*

CONTROL - *That sounds like Hatfield. Not relevant.*

LIEUTENANT - *Wait? What? Hatfield?*

CONTROL - *Have you had direct contact with the phenomena?*

LIEUTENANT - *The enemy? You mean the things that are trying to kill us?*

CONTROL – *Designated term is phenomena.*

LIEUTENANT – *Okay, the phenomena seem to be giant centipedes. Approximately 10 to 15 feet in length, each segment is about a foot to foot and a half, with the upper segments larger. Each segment has one set of claws. It seems to anchor itself and walk about with the first four or five segments, the pinchers anchor into the ground. After that it rears up, and the pincers on the upper segments get huge. No apparent head, except that each segment might have two eyes.*

CONTROL - *We haven't seen that before. Would you say the phenomena is extraterrestrial, extra-dimensional or supernatural?*

LIEUTENANT – *What the fuck?*

CONTROL - Please answer the question.

LIEUTENANT - How should I know?

CONTROL - Any sign of clothing, badges, symbols, tool use, weapons, transport vehicles, any apparent technology at all?

LIEUTENANT - No. No they just run around on their own. Naked. Like M. Night Shyamalan aliens in Signs. Not even pants.

Something bubbles up within the Lieutenant. It could be hysterical laughter. She locks down on it physically.

CONTROL – Probably not extraterrestrial then. Are there any unusual properties? Do they float? Glow? Are they decaying unusually fast?

LIEUTENANT - No, I don't think so. I saw a dismembered specimen. The body parts just seem to sit there.

CONTROL - Sounds like a transdimensional incursion. Seems manageable. Any sign of a wormhole?

LIEUTENANT - What?

CONTROL – Don't worry, if you come across it, you'll know what it is. Sit tight, we'll do a sweep when they finish.

LIEUTENANT - In the meantime, what should I do? Should I look for survivors?

CONTROL - There won't be any survivors.

***

LIEUTENANT (VOICE OVER) - This was hell come to earth. I had no idea why I was here. I had no idea why any of this was happening. Twenty-three hours ago, there was a distress call from the local police, calling for the Army, the National Guard, the Air Force. That wasn't everything.

What Devours Also Hungers – Page 172

***

The Lieutenant is hunkered down behind the remains of a wall. With her are two children. She's decided that her mission is to keep them alive. She needs a mission, because if she doesn't have one, and if it's not keeping these kids alive, then she's just here. Seeing the things she's seen, hearing what she's heard, and it's just mindless chaos. So keep the kids alive, and maybe there's a point to existing.

She lights a match. She's been doing it regularly. The little stick of wood flares brightly like magnesium. When she reported it, control told her that the proportion of oxygen in the air was high. The flame is greenish, which she's told is aerosolized copper, which makes no sense. Sometimes its brighter, sometimes its greener. Wherever the things are from, the rules are slightly different there, and they're spilling over here.

Control keeps telling her to lose the children. She stops listening to orders after a while, though she still reports in.

What Devours Also Hungers – Page 173

The boy is thirteen, he's almost catatonic, unresponsive. His eyes are wider than anyone else's she's ever seen in her life. Circles of white, with irises narrowed to pinpricks. In the scant hour she's been with him, she hasn't seen him blink once. But he answers when he's asked a question, and he does what he's told, so she thinks he's not too far gone.

Or maybe he is.

She thinks there's a scream in him. Waiting. She thinks that if it gets out, then he'll just scream for the rest of his life. That's all he'll ever do. That's going to be all that's left of him, just a scream, going on and on.

The girl is better. She's fourteen. She's carrying the Lieutenants sidearm. It seems to make her feel better, safer. Whatever.

The Lieutenant has an assault rifle. It's not hers. She found it near the ruins of a marine. She wiped the Marine's bits off it, and it seemed serviceable. There was a finger jammed up in the trigger guard, but she'd managed to work it out. It's useless, she knows, the things eat bullets. But like the girl, it makes her feel better. She wishes she had something sharp, something to pry between the chitinous plates of a centipede. She imagines the sound it would make as she worked the blade in and twisted it. She smiles. She can hear it screaming in her head.

Abruptly, she realizes it's not her imagination. Carefully, motioning the children to silence, she creeps to the edge of the ruined wall.

A centipede is screaming. Alien as it is, she can feel its panic. Raw terror exudes from it, it feels like its fear seeps into her pores, it's so pervasive. It's running, out in the open, its multiple limbs churning.

Michaels is behind it, walking calmly, approaching steadily, his mannequin mask devoid of all expression. His dark blue overalls are drenched with green gore.

It turns to look back, at Michaels, and its mouth parts clatter wildly, she can tell it's a squeal. It turns putting on a new burst of speed as it tries to get away. But its limbs tangle over each other and it stumbles. Michaels keeps coming closer. It scrabbles around a corner, Michaels following.

After a moment, there's a wild chitinous screeching. The sound of air being forced through a hundred spiracles, a chain of hearts bursting like a row of firecrackers, segmented limbs torn loose, plates clattering, alien ganglion lighting up with distilled fear.

She turns to the children.

LIEUTENANT - Time to go.

But she has no idea where. Just away. Away from the monsters,

GIRL - Your face.

For a second, the Lieutenant has no idea what she's talking about. But then she flips the reflective visor of her helmet up. It keeps slipping down. She smiles at the children. But they're not reassured.

***

As they crawl through the remains of the town, there are bodies everywhere. She's never seen so many bodies in her life. There is nothing natural or peaceful to any of them, they are torn, mutilated, the corpses are posed. A row of heads adorn a picket fence.

Once crossing the street, they pass the body of a little old lady that had been carefully dissected, first clothes cut away, then

What Devours Also Hungers – Page 175

skin, muscles and bones exquisitely sectioned, intestines and organs laid out. They try not to look, but they can't help it. As they pass, the body turns its head, the jaw works, but there were no lips or tongue. Whatever it wanted to say, the Lieutenant did not know. It doesn't matter anyway.

They startle a small flock of birds which take wing, struggling into the air, then falling to the ground, flopping about. The air is wrong, they couldn't breathe properly.

An automobile caught fire and burns spontaneously, the flame an intense green. They were coming closer, she thought. She should turn around, lead them in the opposite direction.

Or maybe it was just getting stronger.

***

GENERAL - We had a mission in Bakersfield. No big deal. Nest of Vampires. They went in and cleaned it out, like they always do. They killed everyone, of course. There was a group of survivors holed up in the church, it had gotten that bad. Sawyer took the door down with his chain saw. I remember, he stood there a moment. Then he walked in. The saw started up again... And there was just screaming and screaming.

The Lieutenant knows the General is dead. She's proud of her sanity, in the middle of this insane slaughterhouse, as the sky above the centre of town seems to turn a different colour, amidst the bodies and the monsters and the screaming, she's sane. The General is dead. He's not quite a hallucination; he's more than a memory. The children pay no attention, so she tries not to.

GENERAL - They killed the Vampires of course. They killed everyone. That was what they did. After a while, as it was going on, it was as if some of the Vampires were trying to save people. It was strange. It didn't matter, they all died.

What Devours Also Hungers – Page 176

The Lieutenant creeps up to a car. There is a large building in front of a park. City Hall. She is surprised, she had expected a Church, or perhaps some exotic physics lab or power station. There is no cover. Green light shines from the windows. Centipedes are scuttling in and out of the building. They seem uncertain and full of nervousness.

GENERAL - *I was there of course. I made a mistake. This Nosferatu-looking bastard caught me. Corpse skin, rodent incisors, you know that look that they get when they've been around too long, they forget what being human is, it slips away from them. Nosferatu, and he grabbed me with those spidery claw fingers. I thought I was dead. But all he did was say "What have you done? Do you know what you've done? Do you know what you've done?" Over and over, until Vernon killed him. They kill everyone. No one gets away. Nothing stops them. Nothing matters.*

Frustrated, the Lieutenant turns, looking back at the memory.

LIEUTENANT - *What's the point? What's the point of this? Why are you here? Why am I here?*

GENERAL - *You're here to witness. That's your job. You want to save someone, but that's not your job. You won't save anyone.*

The Lieutenant wants to swear at the General, but then she catches the girl looking at her, watching the one sided conversation. She freezes.

She realizes the boy was missing.

***

The boy steps around the corner. He stops, just at the edge. The Lieutenant watched carefully. The boy went up on his tip toes, and then down flat, his knees bend and straighten. His face has no expression, his eyes wide and staring. He waggles his hips, his arms swinging back and forth. For a moment, he seems to be dancing.

What Devours Also Hungers – Page 177

Then his head tilts, his mouth falls open, and blood trickles out. He isn't breathing. He isn't seeing. Vernon, with his doll's mask, steps out, and lets the boy's body slide off the crowbar he'd used to puppet the corpse.

The Lieutenant swears. The girl cowers behind her, but when the Lieutenant reached back to hold her wrist, the girl slipped back a little. Vernon, bored, was already moving on. With effort, she lifts the visor of her helmet so the girl can see she's all right.

But she's not. This is hell, and they are in it.

***

They are in the municipal building. The girl clings to her wrist. The interior is a wreck, gutted. The remains of walls and floors poking from the building's shell. There isn't anything there though.

The Lieutenant had expected something, a wormhole, a glowing portal, a gateway into an other universe, but there was ... nothing. There isn't even a void or some gaping black hole. It is just a kind of non-descript nothingness, an absence that seemed unremarkable. She can't see into it, but it isn't opaque, or diffuse, it isn't light or dark. It just isn't, or it just is, but in an unintrusive way. A casual observer might glance at it; let his eyes linger for a second, and then turn to focus on anything that might be more interesting to look at, because anything was more interesting.

More interesting, like the centipede parts everywhere she looks. They mingle with rotting human corpses. There was an archeological layering in places, ruined and torn human flesh, bodies so thoroughly dismembered they'd lost all significance. And atop them, segmented limbs, chitinous plates, lumps and strips of green gunk, maggot-like worms, a few still squirming, many curled up and dead, or bleeding green

What Devours Also Hungers – Page 178

Whatever was on the other side, it finds this world sour and hateful, unpalatable and repulsive. It loathes this awful place so cold and sour, and yet, it is still unbearably hungry.

They are all there, gathering, Vernon and Michaels, Jackson, Sawyer, Bub, the Smiler, the rest of the men with the masks. Some simply standing, others arriving at their casual unhurried pace.

The girl is gone. What had happened to her? The Lieutenant knew she'd been holding onto her wrist, the grip so tight the Lieutenant's flesh had whitened. Had she? Or had she fled? She had been there. But now she wasn't. Had there been a scream?

The Lieutenant is confused. Time wasn't right. She slides the visor down on her helmet, presenting a red speckled, cracked, reflecting mirror to the world. Somehow it makes her feel right.

A segmented limb advances from the centre of the room, she can't quite see from where. It is narrow and barbed, twisting back on itself in a mantis like claw. It continues to extend, segment after segment after segment, elbows bending this way and that, dozens of twisting segments long, reaching for the men in the masks.

A hooked claw strikes Jackson shaking his massive form. More claws snake and twitch out to the others. Jackson looks down at the claw embedded in his chest, curious. Hairs from the segmented arm beat against his body, wrapped against their forms, sensing, tasting, perhaps seeing in some primitive way.

Jackson snaps the claw off and flings it aside, dismissively. The segmented limbs shiver and writhe in confusion, some of them withdrawing.

Michaels hold his limb, his fist wrapping around a chitinous segment. It jerks in his hand, as if trying to free itself, at first tentatively, and then frantically. The segmented limbs boil suddenly, on flexing convulsive motion. The Lieutenant has the sudden sense that it is trying to get away, as if it is suddenly afraid. As if it has touched something awful.

But it is too late. Michaels holds it in his grip, is walking forward, following it as it shrinks. So is Sawyer, Vernon, all of them walking towards the absence.

Then it is gone. The building is just a gutted building. The light is different, normal; even the air is different, the otherworldliness dissipating like mist. The Men in the Masks, or whatever it was that they were, were gone too. Gone to wherever the other side was.

On her earpiece, control is saying something. It didn't matter. She walks away.

It's over.

***

A couple of days later, the pre-positioned satellite registered activity at the Compound. Seismic sensors registered footsteps. The passive devices ticked over.

The Men in the Masks are back from wherever they had been. No one knew where they had been or how they had returned. They were just there.

***

The Lieutenant sits patiently through debriefing several times. Each round, she finds she has less and less to say. Her responses become monosyllabic. Eventually, she decides she is bored and stops speaking. Sometime after that, she just walks away. She goes home. No one stops her.

What Devours Also Hungers – Page 180

Late that night, she can't sleep. She wakes up, wandering aimlessly around her apartment until the battered flight helmet catches her attention. She picks it up, staring at it, noticing the bloodstains, the flecks of green ichor, the dust and scrapes, the crack along the mirrored visor.

She realizes she is standing naked in front of a mirror, holding it. How had she gotten there? She stares at her face, as if she doesn't recognize it. She looks down at the helmet, and stares at her reflection in the mirrored visor. It looks better there, it looks like it belongs.

She lifts the helmet, and lowers it onto her head, the visor falling into place, reflecting into the mirror, reflecting back, emptiness falling.

It is good.

The End

A Note, Plus More Books by the Author

If you've skipped to the end, looking for an apology, well... Sorry? Also, no refunds.

Thank you for taking the time out to read my little book. If you've made it all the way here, then I'm just going to assume you liked it.

I have a lot more stories, several collections actually. Horror with **Giant Monsters Sing Sad Songs** and There **Are no Doors in Dark Places.** There's comedy and humor with **Drunk Slutty Elf**, a fantasy short story collection.

There are alternate histories – **Fall of Atlantis, Dawn of Cthulhu** and **Bear Cavalry**. Fantasy and altenate history novels like **The Mermaid's Tale** and **Axis of Andes**..

Plus nonfiction about **LEXX**, **Starlost** and **Doctor Who**.

If you liked this, could I suggest you leave a review wherever you got it. Mention it on your blog, or your Facebook. Say nice things. If that's too much, just toss me a couple of stars. Writing is a solitary, lonely pursuit and actually getting some feedback or appreciation is a wonderful thing.

But there's more to it. It's about trying to get out there. There are a lot of people writing a lot of books, and it can get hard to get noticed. Reviews help.

And speaking of writing more....'

Check out my Website, at **denvaldron.com**

HEARTS IN DARKNESS
A Trilogy of Horror Collections

Giant Monsters Sing Sad Songs – The connection between the author of the Necronomicon and a boy in Providence; a girl who meets the last sasquatch; a poet who shares abandoned Tokyo with a Kaiju; and more…

There Are No Doors in Dark Places – A childlike cancer that talks to its owner; A single mother drawn into dark magic; A man who turns into a different monster each night; a vampire that twists lives; a pregnant woman finding her body being stolen from her; and many more

What Devours Also Hungers…

FUNNY FANTASY
and COMIC SCIENCE FICTION

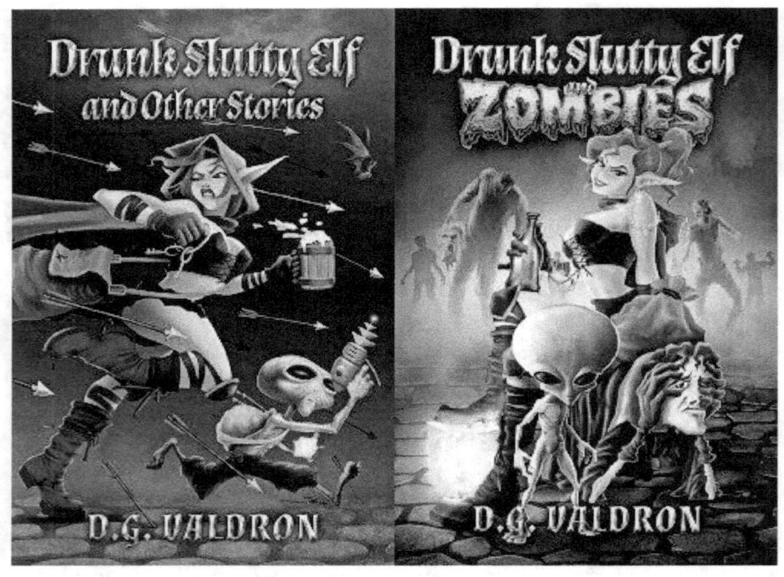

DRUNK SLUTTY ELF AND OTHER STORIES
Plus
DRUNK SLUTTY ELF AND ZOMBIES

Two volumes of savage, satirical, subversive wicked, funny, frantic science fiction and fantasy. Demented ghost hunters, frustrated aliens, horny giants, drunken elves, sneaky ghosts, wayward barbarians and many more.

ALTERNATE REALITIES
A Trilogy or Strange New Worlds
The Other books

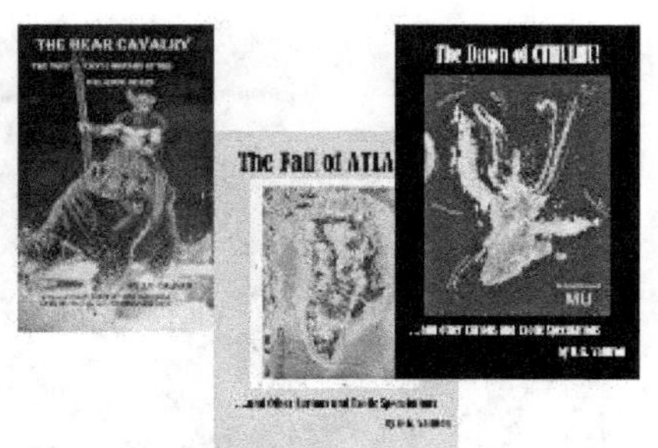

The Dawn of Cthulhu - The Secret History of H.P. Lovecraft's Cthulhu Cult; Lost Continents Found – real and legendary; The Monsters of Sesame Street, is a light hearted examination of Muppets as if they were actual animals.

The Fall of Atlantis – Retroverse, An Accidental Cinematic Universe of 50's Sci Fi movies, Greenland Without the Ice, Rome Crosses the Altantic, and the Rise and Fall of Atlantis, an ecological catastrophe.

The Bear Cavalry, the True (Not!) History of the Icelandic Bears, an off the wall, short novel about the Viking domestication of bears, their evolution into a medieval cavalry Bonus novelette, The Sharebear Apocalypse.

AXIS OF ANDES
NEW WORLD WAR
A History of WWII in South America

Berlin, 1937, Adolph Hitler and his cabinet meet with a strange delegation from Ecuador. The delegates from the small South American nation beg for help, fearing an impending invasion from their rival, Peru. What happens at that meeting sets in motion a chain of events that sets the entire continent on fire. By the time it's done, millions are dead, nations are in ruins, and the map of Latin America will be changed beyond recognition.

A Dark Fantasy of Murder and Redemption

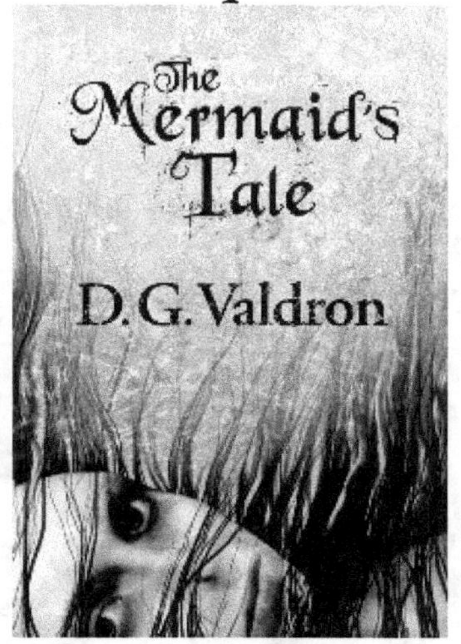

There's a City where all the races come together uneasily, descending into civil war.

There's a Mermaid, murdered cruelly her people distraught and crying out for justice.

There's the Orc, lowest and the worst, her mission: Solve the murder, before it all comes crashing down.

**And there's something else…
…. the world's first serial killer.**

Available only as an Audio Book

What Devours Also Hungers – Page 189

The Pirates Histories of Doctor who

The greatest, most professional Doctor Who fan films ever made, explorations of the peculiarities of copyright, the developments of new technologies, the evolution of fan culture, and histories of the Doctor on stage, in audio, and in animation. These books are full of new and entertaining insights and revelations that you'll love.

What Devours Also Hungers – Page 190

LEXX Unauthorized, the Series

LEXX Unauthorized about the making of a show about a giant space bug that blows up planets, the cowardly security guard who is its captain, and the undead assassin, runaway love slave, and robot head who form its crew.

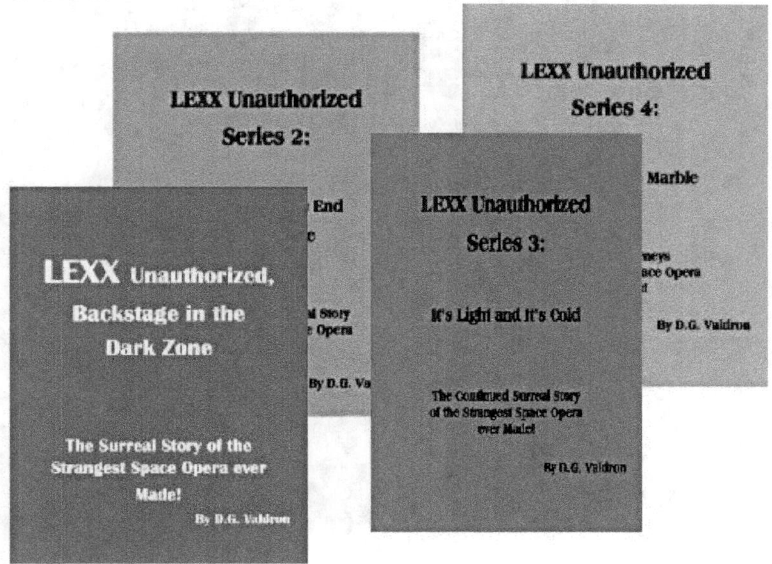

Originally billed as 'Star Trek's Evil Twin,' the cultiest of cult sci fi, LEXX's forte was black humor, startling visuals, big ideas, and a sensibility that had more to do with surrealists like Jodorowsky or Bunuel than mainstream science fiction. And, as unconventional as it was onscreen, the story of how it came to be is even more bizarre.

STARLOST UNAUTHORIZED
And the Quest for Canadian Identity

The series that was Harlan Ellison's nemesis. The most controversial series in the history of sci fi television. This exhaustively researched book, based on interviews with some of the stars and writers, brings a fresh new interpretation of of the Starlost, and a re-evaluation of the series and its themes in the context of the 1970s crisis of Canadian nationalism.

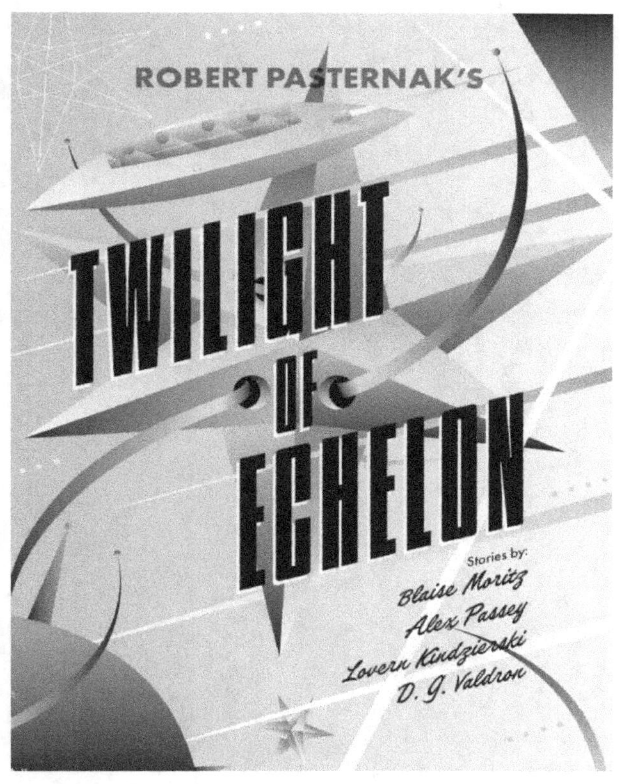

TWILIGHT OF ECHELON
Published by
AT BAY PRESS

Based on the work of famed artist Robert Pasternak the book features paintings from Pasternak's Echelon series, accompanied by stories written independently by D.G. Valdron, Lovern Kindzierski, Alex Passey and Blaise Moritz.

What Devours Also Hungers – Page 193

www.ingramcontent.com/pod-product-compliance
Lightning Source LLC
Chambersburg PA
CBHW060449310726
48977CB00001B/370